Little Shoreham Stories

Bobby Stevenson

ISBN: 9798747532052

Visit @BobbyStevenson on Twitter or
https://randomactsstories.blogspot.com/ or
https://thougthcontrol.wordpress.com/

To the little village of Shoreham, Kent, where amazing things happen.

To all the people who have gone before, to those folks already here, and to those hearts who will one day find the place.

You are the lucky ones.

ON SHOREHAM HILLS

On Shoreham Hills,
I sat a thousand years,
And watched the seasons change
Like fields, from green to brown, to white.
And on those hills,
I saw the Norse arrive and change the way of
things,
Our lives belonged to others now.

On Shoreham Hills,
I watched as paths were walked a
Hundred million times, which turned to
Roads, and streets and lanes,
The poor, the plagued, were taken in
And healed and fed, and given up
To God's own grace.

On Shoreham Hills,
I saw the wooden structures changed to stone
And homes were built to hold those hearts
That felt this secret valley
Theirs to keep.

I sat beside, as William Blake did spy Jerusalem
Among the waters of the Darent streams,
Forever caught by Samuel Palmer's paints.

Then one fine day, the smoke appeared of rail and
train

And in our hearts, we knew those hills were not for
only us.
I lifted eyes to watch the Zeppelin raids on London
Town,
Replaced by Messerschmitt and Spitfire trails.

The buildings rose, as did the streets
Our village grew to meet the age.

I sat on Shoreham Hills, a thousand years
To watch it comfort and console,
And as I watched the sun arise,
I hoped to sit a thousand more.

A PLACE CALLED HOPE

'What makes anyone do anything?'

That was what she thought as she stepped off the bus. She hadn't meant to get off at that particular stop, but the large woman by the window seat had asked to be let out.

The funny thing is that the large woman looked out of the window, tutted, and sat down at another seat. Karen was already standing and so decided that the next stop was as good as any place to leave the bus.

It stopped at the foot of the road leading to the railway station.

At least she could get a train into London if things didn't go well. Whatever those things were that she was planning to do. Goodness knows, she didn't know. Kate hadn't really had time to think. She had just got out of that taxi and was ready to enter the church, where she knew Derek, good old dependable Derek, would be standing at the altar waiting on her.

The thing is, she wasn't prepared to marry a dependable soul. Before she knew it, she had kissed her father on the cheek and then jumped on the first bus that passed.

As she walked down Station Road, she knew one thing – she needed a drink. Good old Derek never drank. He felt that it stopped his dependability.

The first pub she came to was one called the Old George Inn. There were bikers outside, laughing and joking as if the world was a place to live in without problems. Oh, to be one of those people, she thought. Oh, to be among them.

At the next corner was a little pub by the name of the Rising Sun. She decided that this was her spot. This was where she would have a drink.

Inside was a middle-aged woman with a pleasant smile who appeared to be washing her daughter's face. The mother was spitting on her apron, then using that corner to wipe the child's nose and mouth, much to the annoyance of her daughter.

Karen walked to the bar while the woman looked behind Karen to see if anyone else came in with her.

"Just you, then?" Asked the barwoman.

"Is that okay?"

"Sure, hun, sure, we get all sorts in this neck of the woods. Now, what can I get you, dearie?"

Karen asked for a half-pint of ale and sat in the corner by the window. From here, she could see the bridge and the little river.

It was truly unique; the village was surprising, like an iceberg. Shoreham looked a little empty from the road, but once in the centre of the place – it was packed to the brim with life.

"Waiting for someone, are you?" Asked the landlady.

"I don't know what I'm doing," said Karen, and a few tears fell from her face.

"Don't you be crying now, dearie," said the landlady, and she sent her daughter off to find some handkerchiefs.

For the next hour and with no customers, Karen and the landlady chatted about all sorts of things until the woman asked about what had happened earlier that day, and that was when the floodgates opened.

The landlady poured herself half a beer and a brandy for Karen.

"You get that down you, and then we can see what is what. You can stay here tonight if needs be.

Sarah, my daughter, can bunk in with me, and you can take her bed."

And that was how it all started for Karen. She stayed at the Rising Sun, working there at nights and in the afternoons, she waitressed at a tea-room along the High Street.

One day, when she was least expecting it, a farmer came in for a drink and fell in love with Karen in a heartbeat.

I hear that he was nothing like Derek, and they ended up with five children and three grandchildren.

Sometimes, you get off at the stop that was meant.

HECTOR AND THE HONEYPOT

If you ever get the chance to visit the beautiful little village of Shoreham - perhaps by train, or car, or on foot, then I recommend the small tea-room next to what used to be the Royal Oak pub.

The little place has the quaint name of the Honey Pot, and it will sell you beautiful homemade cakes, scones, sandwiches all washed down with a perfect cup of tea or coffee.

The couple who run the place are pleasant and hardworking, resulting in the tearoom becoming very popular. Word of mouth has ensured that the Honey Pot is always packed.

It gets its fair share of ordinary folks just looking for a place to set down their weary selves and enjoy a good natter, but it also attracts the more exotic of the human species. Mostly the couple who work in the shop just smile and move on.

One of those stranger folks was Hector. He was of indeterminate age, and he had grown his hair very long down one side and combed the result over the top of his bald head.

Hector first came into the Honey Pot just to use the bathroom, but as the man behind the counter had told him, one needed to purchase something in order to have a pee. So that is indeed what Hector did. He bought a scone which he ate on the way to the toilet.

Now no one was sure where Hector originated from as his accent was neither here nor there.

Wherever Hector came from, one fact was clear – he was a pest. You see, Hector was probably the best-read man in Kent, perhaps in the island of Great Britain. So you are asking yourself, what has all this got to do with him being a pest in the Honey Pot? Well, I'll tell you.

Hector had read almost every book and every story there was. Okay, I'm exaggerating a little, but you get my drift. He was one smart cookie. And so, it was on a sunny morning when he was walking to Shoreham from wherever it was he lived that he came up with an idea. One that would keep him in cream cakes and tea as long as he liked.

Hector would purchase a cup of tea and nothing else. The man who ran the shop wasn't too happy about the time Hector spent over one cup of tea, but what could he do?

Hector would then wait until a customer of the tearoom took out a book and settled into reading their paperback, novel or whatever – then he would approach them. At first, Hector would make it look as if he were just indulging in a bit of chit-chat, but as he gained their confidence and in a quiet voice, he would whisper, 'buy me a tea and scone or else'.

"Or else what?" Most would ask.
"Or else I'll tell you the ending of that book."
"What, this book?" The shocked customer would say.
"You don't know this book". They would say, but Hector would.

He'd have a rough idea where they were in the book and tell them the story up until that point.

Then he'd threaten to tell the rest of the story. Some got angry and stormed off.

An older man hit Hector on the head with the book and said he hadn't fought in the war to be told the ending of the story. One or two customers – the nervous ones – relented and bought cakes and biscuits for that rascal, Hector.

Then the day came when Hector the Horrible met his match. A kind of rich looking but intelligent gentleman came in for a cream tea *'with all the trimmings'*.

He sat in the corner and began to read from a large book covered in brown paper (the way people did in the 50s and 60s to protect their schoolbooks). It wasn't long before Hector had sidled over to the man and slid into the seat next to him.

"Buy me a cream tea just like you have – with all the trimmings – or I'll tell you the end of the book," said Hector.

"You don't know what I'm reading," responded the man.
"Tell me the title," demanded Hector.
"No," said the gentleman.

Hector was getting a bit desperate, so he changed his tact.
"If I don't guess the end of the book, I'll buy you another cream tea."
"With all the trimmings?" Asked the gentleman.
"With all the trimmings," agreed Hector.
"It's called 'The Life and Times of Millwall Football Club'. So, what's the ending?"

Hector hummed and hawed, and in the end, he shook his head and had to admit defeat.
"I'll have the same again with milk and sugar in the tea. Thank you very much." Said the man.

"So, how does it end?" Asked Hector.
"Why Millwall win the FA cup."

A STREAM WHERE THE OAK TREES GROW

I think I was probably about fifteen summers at the time. I'd been up by the Cross with Harry looking for bits of shrapnel that had fallen from the sky.

This was the summer of 1947, and the sky had started to get blue again, and the world had begun to smile once more.

Harry had been called from the bottom of the hill by his grandfather (who was once a Sergeant-Major in the war) to tell him his meal was on the table and that if he didn't hurry, their dog, Winston, would get it all.

You didn't have to ask Harry twice when it came to food. No sir, he was tumbling and rolling and laughing all the way to the bottom of the grassy slide.

I knew my father would be expecting me around five pm. That was when he got back from the garage in Sevenoaks and would start the cooking. My mother had left me, my brother and my dad in the war and had never returned. She didn't die if that's what you're thinking. She ran away with a soldier from Philadelphia, and that was that.

I saw the man coming out of the sun as it finally dipped behind the woods above the Cross. In that light, he looked like Father Christmas – if Father Christmas had been on his holidays in Shoreham. I mean, it was still only the first few days of August.

"Do you mind if I sit here?" He asked, and I nodded because I was too busy trying to capture a butterfly with my hands. In those days, long ago, you spoke to strangers – before people grew afraid of each other. Perhaps they are right to be scared; I honestly couldn't tell you one way or another.

The man with the beard sat next to me and smiled. He looked out over the valley and the river and said, "Well, aren't you the lucky one?".

To be honest, I wasn't sure what he meant – but thinking back now over the years, I guess he was right; those beautiful hills and the river Darent – we were lucky and should never, ever take them for granted.

"You know what they call that river?" He asked.

"The river Darent, sir." I said as he smiled at my use of the word 'sir'.

"Well done, lad, well done. The Celts called it after the 'stream where the oak trees grow', and even the Anglo-Saxons called it Diorente. It is a special place. Magical."

"What do you mean 'magical'?" I asked. Well, I had to ask, I was fifteen, for goodness sake. Curiosity was in my blood.

"This river, this valley, this village below, all of them make up a healing place."

"They do?"

"They certainly do."

"Folks never find Shoreham." Then he laughed until I thought his head was going to fall off (or explode). "Shoreham finds them," he said when he'd quietened down.

"It does?"

"Yep."

"This little village has taken people in since the dawn of time. It used to take in plague victims, lepers, the poor, and the sick. And it always took care of them until they left, one way or another. You ask your mum or dad about how they or their family found Shoreham, and you'll find there's always for a reason, usually a strange reason."

He said, delighted with himself. "You see, Shoreham hears people's hearts. It knows if they need something, and it takes them in. These folks think they came here accidentally – but that's not true. The truth is, the village knows you're hurting or that something bad will one day happen to you, and it makes sure you are within its care when it does." He looked at me to see if I was taking all this in, and to be honest, I was.

"One day, when you are ready, you'll go out into the world and be happy. Some people find this village late in life, but that doesn't mean they don't need it just as much as anyone else. It heals them, listens to them, finds companions for folks, and when their hearts are ready, it sends them on their way."

It was then that I knew, from the tickling in my palms, that I had caught the butterfly and decided perhaps I should let the little thing go. As it flew up into the darkening blue sky, I turned to tell the old man – but there was no one there.

And you know what? This place did heal my family. My father married again and moved to Hasting. My father's newly found happiness spread to us all, and we kept together as a loving group, and maybe it was all thanks to that little village. Shoreham.

You never, ever find Shoreham. It finds you.

THE STALK EXCHANGE

If I had started the story, 'once upon a time' it might have given me more leeway with the tale that lies ahead - but the bottom line, the very bare-knuckled truth about it all, is that everything described in this story is the God's honest truth, may I be struck down and turned to stone if it ain't so.`

When did it take place? You might ask. Well, not as long ago as you would have imagined, and yet not so close that you might have known the folks involved.

It all started in the dying days of one hot summer in a village in Kent. A hamlet that cowered beneath a white cross, with its several pubs, a dainty tea-room and every shade of human being that inhabited God's imagination.

The heroine, or the hero, depending on your take of this world, was an old maid (if one can be described as such) by the name of Rosetta Stone – I kid you not – and I'm sure she had heard every take on that subject until it had bubbled up through her head and blew, gushing, out the very top like a giant whale.

What was important and just as crucial with every soul who walks this Earth is what makes a heart tick. For let me tell you right now, in case you are in any doubt, she was the very best of folks, and this was in a gentler, kinder time when the world still hadn't faced up to its cruelty.

She lived and breathed, and loved and hoped, and possibly all in equal measures. She had no reason to be such a wonder, for the folks who had brought her into this world were not as kind as Rosetta – that love had jumped a generation - and for all her missed starts in life, Rosetta was who she was, and that was plain for everyone to see.

She had found love two and a half times in her former days – which had been enough for her. Rosetta had never expected to find love – not at all - but it had come looking for her, and she had not found it wanting. Now Rosetta was alone – an old maid – as I have already told you. It wasn't a description that caused her any concern – and to be honest, she wore the title with a bit of pride and a little sadness.

Now that we know who the story is about, I will tell you 'what' the story also involves.

In the very centre of this little village was an old red telephone box. It had been the very focal point of communications for all points outside the area many generations ago. Folks would queue on warm Friday evenings outside the telephone box to get their share at talking to a mother, father, lover or pal. Perhaps sometimes the person waited on the friend to call them and with a bit of tutting from those waiting in the queue – a lonely heart would jump, as the telephone in the box rang out in all its splendour.

Eventually, as it must, the world and science took over, and people had found other ways to talk to each other, and thus the little red box grew cold and lonely and forgotten.

One winter's evening, a gentleman from the telephone company came to the village and ripped the very heart out of the telephone box (or just the plain box as it was now known).

Very little happened to it. Maybe a child who ran away from home was found in it, or perhaps an old drunk, on the way to somewhere else, had sheltered in it – and so, it was decided to demolish the old red box and put it out of its misery.

This caused Rosetta to be rather sad, and so she made up her mind to find a use for the structure. Wasn't this a place she had talked to lovers? At least, before those lovers had left her to face old age alone.

One morning she potted up some of her plants which she had grown from her sweat and tears in her little garden, and put them in the telephone box. She left a note telling anyone interested to help themselves to the plants or cuttings. And it was precisely this that the visitors to the box did. Except a funny thing occurred - some left plants in return. Some left flowers, others left cuttings, all to thank Rosetta for her kindness.

It was because of this that the box became known as the Stalk Exchange. It was now somewhat famous and was even covered in a local newspaper during a week when there was very little news.

One day, when Rosetta was collecting gifts and leaving more plants, an old man happened to stop by. His name was Michael, and he was a widower.

He had read about Rosetta and her flower exchanges and had wanted to bring one of his wife's favourite plants. Since his wife had died – something he could not still accept – he had found himself at a loose end and had decided to see more of the world. So, Michael had travelled thirty-five miles by train to come to the little village below the Cross.
Rosetta thanked him and asked if he wanted to share some tea she had in her flask.

And that is how it all began. Week by week, people came to see the plants, to share their cuttings and flowers and, more importantly, their stories with

Rosetta. She had two chairs by the old red box and a flask of hot tea on standby.

People came to laugh, to cry, some of the village children came to talk about their problems or even ask for help with their homework.

And one could almost imagine the little red phone box smiling in the sunshine – and Rosetta, well, she was no longer an old maid in the dusk of her life.

She had found more friends and more flowers than she could have ever hoped, and the world had grown a little brighter.

THE SHOREHAM WILD ONES

I suppose it all started on that wet Wednesday, at the cinema on St John's Hill. Mavis had been walking up towards town when it had started to rain and had nothing to keep her head dry.

Mavis had never been into one of those racy films before, certainly not one with an X certificate, but she liked the look of the star on the poster. He seemed strong and mean in his leather jacket: the film was called The Wild One, and the star was someone called Marlon Brando.

So Mavis gave up her money and sat with three other soaked people in the cinema hall. If Mavis were being honest with herself, she would have to say that she was rather excited.

Firstly, she'd never been to the cinema on her own, Bert always took her (God rest his soul), and he would certainly never have approved of a film called 'The Wild One'. Still, what no one knew about her wouldn't hurt them. Just to make sure, Mavis looked around, confident that there were no friends up to the same shenanigans.

By the time the film had finished, she felt all peculiar and put it down to the chocolate ice cream she had eaten. What she couldn't get out of her mind was thought of her in a leather jacket on a motorcycle. This idea persisted with her all the way home on the bus.

When she got into her house, she pulled the curtains - just in case anyone passing by could guess what she was up to, then turned Bert's photo towards the wall as a precaution.

Mavis decided that night that she wasn't going to her grave until she had ridden on a motorcycle while wearing a leather jacket. The tricky thing was to find out who had a bike

She had often seen bikers sitting drinking outside the George pub, and so Mavis decided to sit with her orange drink and wait for one of them to stop by. Like all best-laid plans, a biker and his girlfriend had just stopped at the pub just as Mrs Lightfoot came over to ask Mavis if she would help her arrange the flowers in the church. Of course, Mavis couldn't refuse. She could hardly tell Mrs Lightfoot that she was waiting on a biker.

Plan B was to knit herself a jumper with the slogan 'Hell's Angels' on the front. It took her several days, and when she'd finished, she felt quite giggly and had a small sherry to settle herself down.

Mavis found her Grandfather's old pushbike, which had lain in the garden shed for as long as she could remember. She went to the library and took out a book called 'Bicycle Maintenance for Beginners'. It was ever so helpful, and within a couple of days, she had the old bicycle back on its wheels again.

On her first excursion, she waited until it was dark before pulling on her jumper. She pushed the bike to the top of Church Street and proceeded to freewheel all the way down. All she was missing was Marlon Brando, and she would be good to go.

The next day there was talk in the village shop of strange sounds in the night: 'it sounded like a banshee,' said one. Another was sure that there was a crazy biker riding through the village at night trying to scare the good folks. Mavis overheard one of these conversations and was about to tell all when she suddenly thought of a better idea.

The following week it was her turn to hold the Village Knitting and Sewing Night at her home. It was also her turn to provide a pattern that the good folks of the knitting Bee could follow.

On that evening - after she had plied them with more than the usual amount of sherry - she went into her bedroom and returned wearing her 'Hell's Angels' jumper.

Mrs McLarttey nearly fell off her seat, but the rest of them seemed to like what she was wearing. Perhaps they would feel different in the morning when the sherry wasn't controlling their thoughts as much. Yet, one by one, she talked them all around to knitting themselves the same jumper.

During the weeks that it took to complete the work, Mavis still freewheeled her bike down Station road, around into Church Street and over the bridge, all the time shouting *'whee'* as she went. She couldn't recall Marlon Brando shouting *'whee'*, but she was sure he would have, had Marlon been doing what Mavis was doing.

Each week she would tell the gang a little more of her story about the Wild One and about her fixing up her Grandfather's bike.

By the time the jumpers were ready, so were the ladies. One quiet, dark night, they all pushed their bicycles up to the top of Station Road, whipped on their 'Hell's Angels' tops and *'whee'd'* their way all down the road into the street and over the bridge.

None of them had ever felt more alive.

Some of the biker ladies were present at the Parish Council Meeting when Mr Hotten brought up the complaint about the gangs that had recently started invading 'our quiet little village'. He banged his fist on the table and said something must be done and quickly. Mr Hotten felt that a spell in the army might do the offenders a world of good.

Some of the gang tutted, shook their heads, and then winked at each other.

They knew the truth, and they weren't going to tell anyone. After all, weren't these ladies - the Shoreham Wild Ones?

THE SHOREHAM NIGHT CAFÉ

It wasn't planned, nor had it been meant. It had just happened, much like the start of the universe at the Big Bang.

Treacle (actually, she was Christened, Ann, but no one had ever really called her that) still had one set of keys to the village hall door. She was eighty years of age and still very sprightly, as some folks were want to say. She had cleaned the hall, girl and woman, for the last sixty-one years, and still, she found herself nipping in from time to time to check if the place was its usual pristine self.

If it wasn't, she would straighten a curtain here or wipe a smudge there, but usually, she found that she had taught the younger folks well and that they had all done an excellent job.

When Treacle lost her Harold, after he had a long battle with Alzheimer's, she found her life as empty as an enormous hole in the world. For the last eight years, she had watched the love of her life take a long and slow walk into oblivion. She couldn't say when the man she loved had properly left, but it was the longest goodbye of her life.

She neither cried nor complained. What was the point? Everyone was walking around with some burden on their shoulders. Hers was a burden of love.

One Tuesday morning, she awoke as she always did around 3.24 am. It was always there or thereabouts – Treacle couldn't help wondering if there was some significance to that time on the clock.

It was a warm Spring morning, and the Sun would be rising sooner rather than later. So, Treacle got dressed and wandered down to the village hall. She knew there would be something there to keep her occupied – to help her stop thinking about Harold.

When she stepped inside, a few bits and pieces were left scattered from the Kid's Club, and very quickly, she had those tidied away.

"I'll just make a cup of tea," she said out loud to Harold, hoping he was listening.

She had found an old digestive biscuit on one of the shelves and was about to sit down to enjoy her cuppa when there was a tap at the door. She looked at the clock; it said 4.17 am. Perhaps it was the police.

Treacle moved along a few windows to see if she could see who was at the door. She recognised the silhouette, and it was old Tommy from across the High Street.

Tommy had been a widower for many a year and had accepted it all – like he did life – with a stiff upper lip.

"Hello Tommy, what brings you here at this time?"

And Tommy explained that he'd seen the light on in the hall and wondered what was up. It was Tommy who had said about the village that if you put on your bathroom light twice in one night, some neighbour would call an ambulance for you.

Treacle made Tommy a cup of tea, and they shared a digestive biscuit. They didn't talk about anything in particular, and most of the time, they didn't talk at all. It was just lovely to have another human to sit with in the wee small hours of the morning.

The following night, Treacle woke around the same time and once again, she was down the village hall and once again, Tommy knocked on the door. This time Tommy brought his dog with him.

"Seems a shame to leave him in on his own."

Treacle had bought newer biscuits – ones with chocolate on top – and both she, Tommy, and Elvis the dog shared them.

The following night, Tommy was disappointed to see that the hall was in darkness and later found out that Treacle had gone to visit her daughter.

By the time that Treacle got back to the hall again, Tommy had been talking to others about the night-time meetings, and when Treacle sat in the hall at 3.30 am – there was a knock on the door and Tommy, his dog, and seven other people joined them.

It seemed that many people in the village found it difficult to sleep. A couple of them played cards. One or two just sat and talked about this and that. One lady, whose husband was fighting overseas, sat and knitted his Christmas presents.

At the end of the month, Treacle was opening the hall three nights a week, and about a dozen people were coming in at any one time: people who found the dark of night the loneliest time in their lives.

The blackness always made demons and problems seem ten times their size and leave the soul empty and dark. No one could fight their night problems – folks would have to wait for the return of the sun to be able to stand again.

But the club, The Lonely Soul Night Café (as Tommy called it), started to attract young and old. Edward, who had lost his dad a few years earlier, still had

night sweats and found that talking to other hearts
sometimes took the pain away a little.

Bernadette, who had always liked a little sherry to
help her sleep, found that there was more warmth
and kindness in the night café than at the bottom
of a glass.

They even started to put on little plays, and folks
would write a poem or a song, or perhaps they
would just stand and say how they were feeling
that particular week. Maybe they were missing
their love-heart, or their children, or regretting
chances they had missed in life. Whatever it was, it
was spoken and dealt with at the café.

Some folks started to find that they made it
through to the morning without wakening. For
some, they felt sad they had missed another night
at the hall.

But for most, it meant that their healing was
starting, and they were ready to face the world
again.

And that was everything.

SHOREHAM, CHRISTMAS, 1944

There is a village, called Shoreham, in the southeast of England which stands alone in many ways. None more so than during the years of World War 2 when every building sustained some bomb damage.

In this little hamlet, the folks were, and are, made of stouter stuff, and for every injury inflicted on the village, the hearts and minds of the villagers came back twice as strong.

I have to say that the place of which I write is nestled in hills below the metropolis of London, and like a little brother standing under the protection of an older one, sometimes the punches thrown at the city also landed on the village.

Shoreham had waved farewell to many souls over the war years, and some of those good folks had not returned, some would never return, and so, some saw the village through sadder hearts and eyes.

Many would never speak of what they had seen, except to nod to a fellow soldier on the way to church on a Sunday morning, and in that nod, they knew what each was thinking. In their minds, there was no point in fighting a war for freedom then burdening loved ones with stories of hate and guilt.

In December 1944, the village folks were beginning to tire of the constant war and had decided to hold a Christmas party in the village hall. Food was rationed, but the fields and gardens of the hamlet had been used to grow some treats for such a party. Each of the villagers sacrificed a little food here and there, and a local farmer donated two chickens to the affair.

There was talk of hope in everyone's hearts that this would be the final Christmas they spent at war. The enemy was beginning to withdraw from all areas of Europe, and there was a feeling that the end would be coming soon.

The village men were few and far between, so one of the residents Old Harry, who had been to two wars in his day, was chosen to be Father Christmas.

Residents had made gifts from all sorts of scraps of material, wood, dried flowers, and even old presents no longer needed. It was the children who were important, and it was for the children that the toys and gifts were made.

That afternoon, the afternoon of the party in the village hall, a little flurry of snow started to fall. The Cross on the hill, which had been covered over for the period of the war, could be seen in outline as the snow settled on it.

The children were given one sweet each, and as they excitedly sucked on them, they sat in a well-behaved line waiting on Santa.

Old Harry was meant to arrive at 2 pm, but by 2.15, there was still no sign of him. Gladys, who had taken it upon herself to organise the party (it kept her mind off her son who had been taken prisoner in the Far East), decided to send Edith to fetch Old Harry as she didn't want the children to be disappointed.

The snow was beginning to fall heavily, and the village sky grew darker. Soon the warden would be doing his rounds and expecting the village black-out curtains to be pulled tightly shut.

At 2.30 pm, there was still no sign of Santa, and Gladys wondered if perhaps she could get away with dressing up as Santa herself.

Just then, Santa arrived in the village hall, covered in snow and with a bag full of colourful presents.

One by one, the children sat on Santa's knee and told him what they wanted for Christmas. Nearly all of them said the same thing: they wanted their daddy, or brother, or sister, or mother to return home for Christmas day.

Each child took a toy, and each child seemed to enjoy what they had been given.

At 3.10 pm, Santa said goodbye and told the children that he'd parked his sleigh up by the Cross and that his reindeer would be missing him. Gladys made a little speech, and the children were all made to say 'thank you, Santa' – even although they were more interested in their gifts.

At 4 pm, Gladys had just finished tidying up the hall when Edith came running in. She said she was sorry about what had happened, that she had got no answer from Old Harry's house and had asked the local constable to break in.

It seems that Harry had died in his sleep and was stone cold by the time they found him. Edith asked if the children were disappointed, and Gladys said that Harry had shown up and given out the gifts.

"You mean these ones?" Asked Edith.

Sure enough, the presents they had made for the children were still lying in the baskets at the back of the hall.

SHOREHAM UNITED

In their heyday, they could have taken on anyone. The team played on and off for over a hundred years (obviously not the same people). Every Saturday when the football team played at home, a good crowd of 10 to 12 people would show up to cheer them on.

The pitch they played on (and by pitch, I mean one that was on a slope of 30 degrees) was situated behind the pretty little village school. The slope ran down from west to east and was so steep that kids used to tell stories of how Edmund Hillary had used it to train on it before he took on Everest.

This football had gone on from Victorian times; fathers played for the team, then sons, then grandsons and so on. Nothing untoward ever happened – that was until Shoreham were drawn against a team of ruffians. Rascals to a man from a town near the river Thames (and that's as much as needs to be said on that topic). This team caused ructions everywhere they went. It was said that at least two of them were in jail at any one time, several were on probation, and the rest hadn't been caught yet.

This team (who shall not be named) progressed through the Kent cup with an unholy ease due to their opponents either not turning up or, if they did, they tended not to put up much of a resistance.

Yes, they were bullies, and it served them well.

When the news broke that Shoreham United were playing against that team, the village decided to have a meeting that very evening in the school. It was more a way of devising a war strategy than anything else more constructive.

The football management consisted of two of Shoreham's best – there was 'The Singer' and 'The Plumber'.

The Singer (who was the older of the two) opened the meeting by asking that time-old question:

"What the hell are we going to do?"

"Well, boss," said one of the strikers, "aren't you better asking, who wants to play?".

"Okay, who wants to play?" Asked The Singer while humming a tune.

Not one person put their hands up.

"No one?"

Everyone dropped their heads. Most of them had been told by their girlfriends/wives/mothers that if they played and then came back battered, there would be trouble.

"So, who are you more scared of?" Asked The Plumber. "Your wives or this team?"

Everyone had to be honest and state that it was a difficult question – either way, they were on to a loser.

"Better not to play, boss than the alternative."

Everyone nodded their heads.

This state of affairs annoyed The Singer, who then broke into a song (in an attempt to inspire the troops). He had chosen the song wisely, one of the latest chart-topping songs (well, a hit twenty years ago), and he sang it at the top of his voice.

The Plumber started banging on the water pipes with his wrench telling the team that this was their D-Day. If they let the team (who shall not be named) tread on them, those cheats would lift the trophy. It couldn't be allowed to happen.

"We shall fight them on the beaches," cried The Plumber, and the team all stood and clapped, just like they did on Strictly (not the team, they had never been on Strictly).

It wasn't long before the great day was upon them.

The team from near the Thames brought a great support of people whose facial parts weren't necessarily in the same place they had been when they were born. Shoreham, itself, had whipped up a great support of twenty-three souls – the largest crowd ever seen at the home ground.

As you can imagine, no one wanted to be the referee. Who would? In days leading up to the game, The Plumber had held a raffle and sold it to the village that it was a privilege to be selected. The winner would be the Ref. Luckily it went to someone who only knew a bit about football – and he was also the man who managed a local hostelry.

The referee agreed to do the job on two conditions. One – that The Singer was not allowed to sing anywhere near him, and two, he could be allowed to sit in his car.

And that is what happened. The referee sat in his car at the side of the pitch.

Flashing his headlights meant he had blown his whistle, and indicating left or right meant which team had been involved in whatever it was.

When the referee called the first foul, it was against that un-named team – one of their players had gone off the pitch, picked up a piece of wood and hit the Shoreham player.

It was just then that the referee realised he hadn't locked his car doors. So that is what he did immediately when he saw the whole of the away team coming towards him.

They rocked his car and asked him nicely to change his mind because it wasn't a foul. The referee thought he might have got some support from the home team, but through the gaps of the 'folks who were rocking his car', he could see Shoreham United all having a smoke of their cigarettes. The Singer was singing something at the top of his voice, and The Plumber was attempting to forge his pipes into weapons.

Some of the Shoreham supporters came over and pulled the team away from the referee's car. Once they had done that, they managed to get the Ref's car the right way up again.

Then it happened. That team who shall not be named gave away a penalty, and it was a penalty. Their goal-keeper had punched the Shoreham striker as he approached the goal-mouth.

Everyone stopped and looked at the referee. The referee was sure he was having a heart attack – his heart was pumping so hard through his pink Angora sweater.

Some might call it justice, others might call it having a break-down, but the referee started up his engine and drove his car at the team that should not be named. He chased them all around the mountainside (or the home pitch, as it is called) and out into the car park.

That team jumped into their own cars and drove off.

Everyone involved with Shoreham United cheered and quickly retired to the new changing hut for lashings of ginger beer.

A great night was had by all, as by default Shoreham United were through to the next round of the cup.

That evening, everyone left the changing hut happy and in high spirits. Only The Singer (who had been tied to a pipe and his mouth taped over) was still there at the end of the night.

SPIRITS AT THE KINGS ARMS

A while back, he wouldn't have been having a conversation about all of this, but a while back, the world was a different place.

All his life, he'd been an eccentric little kid, and for that read - he'd done his own thing. Sometimes being that way meant folks either took longer to catch up with you, never managed to catch up with you, or couldn't be bothered to try. That was fair enough; aren't we are all only living a life ruled by what we know and see.

He had studied sciences and was more down-to-Earth than just believing in the unknown – or whatever it's called these days.

One sleepless night, his mind went back to those initial three days in that house in Surrey. A place he had rented because of work – in those days, he was working on a drug to help with prostate cancer – a drug, by the way, that his father was now taking due to his ill-health – 'the circle of life', he thought.

The house had several floors and five bedrooms, and he had only rented it because there was a full-size set of goalposts in the back garden. The firm he had worked for had given him the money to rent the place.

He remembered it all as if it were yesterday. That first night in the front bedroom, the place had grown ice-cold, then at 1 am, the telephone in the bedroom had rung. When he eventually got up to answer it, there was no one there. As he returned to bed, a smoke detector in the hall began to beep – he lay for a while, ready to get up and fix it, but the next thing he knew was that it was morning.

On the second night, all those things happened again – the telephone ringing, the coldness, the smoke detector (he meant to check the thing but went to work instead).

After a third night of the ice-cold room, the calls and the beeping, he decided to check the smoke detector. It was lying underneath a radiator, and he imagined this is what had caused the beeping to begin – it didn't explain why it happened at the hour it did. He lifted the small smoke alarm only to find that it was missing a battery. In a split-second, he felt as if perhaps the house didn't want him in that room, and for the rest of the stay in the rented house, he lived out of a small side bedroom.

Everything stopped—all the weird stuff.

He'd once, as a sort of joke, attended a psychic night at a friend's house. Due to illness, someone couldn't attend that night, and he'd been asked to make up the numbers. When the woman arrived, she just let out a scream and left the building. Her husband (who was her sort of support) apologised to everyone and went on his way. Although (and it's only put in without suggesting anything) – the couple who were responsible for organising the night both died relatively young.

So now he was where we was. He was working the occasional shift in the Kings Arms for reasons too long to explain.

He hadn't noticed anything, not at first. Then one day, when the pub was empty, and the last lunchtime customer had gone, he saw a man walk up to the side bar.

"How can I help you?" He asked but was surprised to find that there was no one there. 'They must have gone to the toilet', he thought to himself. Soon some walkers came in and distracted him.

A few weeks later, he noticed a customer sliding around to the back bar, and so he hurried up to help - but when he got there, once again, no one was there.

The visitations grew in number, but mostly when the pub was quiet. The figure always headed to the same corner of the room. To him, it was either a sign that he was growing old and losing his marbles or something benign was inhabiting the bar.

He asked around, and several of the staff and customers had all said they'd seen something, always in the same area of the bar. The figure would end up sitting in the corner of the pub.

It was just before Christmas, one Saturday afternoon when the snow was heavy, that it happened. He'd gone outside to clear up some glasses – yes, some people loved to sit outside in this nose-clearing, sharp air.

He didn't see the car skidding across the bridge and slide into the seats in front of the pub.

The car hit him hard in his back and mowed him down. Yet he seemed fine when he came around. He stood up, brushed the snow from himself and checked everything was intact.

Some of the regular drinkers ran past him and out to the car. He was about to tell them that he was okay when he turned around.

There, lying under the car, was a body. His body - with his face - and the village folks were trying to revive him.

He wanted to tell them there must be some kind of mistake. Wasn't he standing beside them, feeling brilliant?

He felt a little shaky with it all and so headed into the pub to sit in the corner and try to work out what had happened.

"He's dead," was what he heard from outside the door.

"He's dead."

SHOREHAM AND THE FOOTBAZOOTS

I think it was Mrs Broadstairs who first saw the lights in the sky and decided it was the Three Wise Men on a comeback tour. She had just purchased (guiltily, I might add) her annual bottle of sherry from the village shop when she happened to step outside to see a large, searing light heading towards the hills behind her.

"Well, I'll be." She muttered to herself. "It's a bit late in the year for fireworks; perhaps it's those Wisemen on a comeback tour" - (see, I told you that's what she'd think).

Of the four people who witnessed the lights in the sky that night, three assumed it was those pesky kids, but not Billy Arnold. Billy had always had a curious nature – 'It killed the cat, and it'll it will get you one day, you mark my words,' – said his mother, who would never die of curiosity on account that she was too lazy to worry about anything.

When Billy told the story later, he remarked that the weird folks had said,' take me to your leader' or something similar, he wasn't sure if that was true, or he had seen it on Doctor Who.

But Billy was confident that they had said that they were from the planet 'Huge Lump' and that they were known as the 'FootBazoots'.

He wasn't sure which was which of the first two he was introduced to, but to the one with the three eyes, he shook the claw and said, 'You are welcome to Shoreham, Mr FootBazoot, and you too, Mrs FootBazoot' (he shook the leg of that one when it was offered).

Now apparently - and this is Billy for you – as he told his story in every pub in the village (mainly for a free drink) – the story got larger and weirder.

Still, the one point that he had made clear to everyone was that the Aliens had mistaken the Cross on the hill for a landing site.

Their leader on Big Lump (their planet) had told them to expect a large cross to mark where they should put down their ship, and this would be the point where they would take over the Earth and enslave all and sundry. Billy said they had definitely said 'Sundry', but he wasn't sure who or what they were. Maybe people from Sundridge?

Their demands were simple. The village of Shoreham was to send their worst singer before the Moon set again, and the FootBazoots would move on to their actual landing site.

The Shoreham Village council spent all night trying to work out who was the worst singer in Shoreham – they had got the list down to 35 names (from 107). But who of those could they sacrifice? They got that list down to 35, too.

When they did eventually choose one name (and it was down to the fact that that person owed one of the Parish Council members some money) – the poor soul was sent up to the Cross to appease the FootBazoots and their evil empire.

When the worst singer (who shall not be named in this story) of Shoreham returned (alive), he started to chuckle. He said that apparently, what Billy heard was 'Werst Sanger', which was FootBazootian for a Very Intelligent Person.

Now they had real problems. Where could they find one of those in Shoreham?

THE HEART ACADEMY

That long hot summer of 1927, which now seems lost in the past, felt then as if it had lasted forever. Folks took cover under trees and left feet dangling in streams while the kids ran barefoot along the riverbanks, throwing stones at imaginary creatures.

As Jake made his way down into the valley, he noticed how the sun had bleached most of the wooden posts. This was Jake's life now, not that it was much of a life, but it kept him reasonably happy. The ironic thing was that he had survived the war, the Great one, that is, while his fiancée had not.

He had never really heard about Shoreham, not until Helen had started working in the shop on the High Street. She was fourteen when she took on the job, and Jake would walk every day after his work to meet her and walk her back to her home; fifteen miles in all, but that didn't bother him, he was with his favourite girl, and that's all that mattered.

When the time came, Jake and his pals all went to war together: all feeling alive and believing that seeing the world would be the start of a new life for them all.

Jake and his mate, Johnny, were the only two who came home. Johnny had lost his sight at the Somme and eventually moved to Birmingham to live with his aunt. Jake's darling, and the love of his life, Helen, got caught in a Zeppelin raid in 1915.

Jake arrived in the year 1927 via three marriage proposals (all refused) and with a business of painting and repairs – one which he had built up from scratch and which now employed three other men. Men were in short supply after the war, and Jake did well to hold on to his guys.

Although he was doing okay financially, he was still lonely and missing his love Helen, and that is why, once a month, Jake would walk from his home in South London to the village of Shoreham – to relive the walks he made in the old days.

On one of those hot, hot days in 1927, Jake found himself walking past the Shoreham Village Hall, and from inside, he could hear someone shouting:

"Damn and blast, blast and damn," said the gruff voice.

The words belonged to Alex Green, a rough man in his sixties, who was trying to move a block of wood and failing very badly.

"Damn, damn, damn," he shouted again. This time a lady of a similar age shouted from the stage.

"Quiet, Alex, the Lord can hear you."

"I don't care if he can. He ain't helping me with this scenery, now is he?"

Jake had found himself in the middle of the village hall, and this was the home to the Players – they had only been in existence for a couple of years, but already they were bringing a smile and some warmth back to the community.

When Alex spotted Jake, he felt that maybe the Lord had been listening after all.

"Here, grab this," shouted Alex, as if he were still in the army.

Jake did as he was told and grabbed the end of the plank.

By the close of the afternoon, Jake had moved scenery, repaired some curtains, and had helped in painting a cloth at the rear of the stage, and do you know what? He had enjoyed it all. Every minute of it.

"Might see you next week, then?" Asked Alex.

Jake nodded and meant it. On the way home, as Jake walked past Helen's old shop, he smiled, whispered 'thanks', and walked up the valley faster than usual.

All that Jake could think about that following week was his walk to Shoreham and the work that would be waiting on him there. For the first time in a very long time, people needed him.

The next Saturday, Jake suggested a particular piece of scenery and how it could be improved. There were six people in the hall that day, and they all voted on the spot to take on board Jake's changes.

At the end of the month, the play was put on the stage, and Jake came down to sit and admire his handy work. He laughed and cried at the play and enjoyed watching the folks of the village entertaining their friends. It was all this incredible stuff that built villages.

When the play was over, Jake felt lost, as if something important had been taken away from him. So, he filled his weekends with walks to and from Shoreham. Sometimes he sat by the Cross on the Hill and talked to his sweetheart Helen – he was sure she was always up there waiting on him.

One cold Saturday afternoon in November, Jake noticed a light on in the village hall. As he entered, he could hear Alex cursing and swearing about something or other. When Alex saw Jake, he smiled.

"I was going to send a letter to your place asking if you wanted to help on this new play, then I realised I had no idea where you lived," said Alex.

Jake slapped Alex on the back, and they chuckled.

That Christmas, Jake didn't sit in the audience, but instead, he helped backstage - and as he looked out at the faces all laughing and enjoying the evening, he smiled to himself and felt that he'd finally found a home.

WOODROW FROM SHOREHAM

Here's the strange thing, no one was ever really sure when Woodrow moved to the village. You must remember him? He lived in that little cottage at the top of Mill Lane. His lounge window faced onto the High Street and was always full of jolly trinkets.

You see, if you asked a neighbour when they remember Woodrow coming here, they'd say – 'Oh, he's always lived here', and someone else might have uttered – 'I think he moved to Mill Lane last Christmas or was it last month?'.

It's not as if he was a mysterious soul, far from it. He was always the life and soul of every party. And if you looked back at photographs, he would be in them.

Woodrow was my pal, and my mentor and my everything at the time. I was barely ten, and I believed that he was so old that he had probably been to school with God.

I asked him once how old he was, and he just chuckled a bit and then said that he was a gnat's hair older than his teeth. Then he'd laugh so hard and loud and long that I could hear his tummy rumble, and at which point he'd say, 'well...excuse me, little one'.

Everyone had a Woodrow story, and every one of them was as different as they were strange.

My story was to do with a gift from that kind man.

Woodrow had a box on top of his fireplace, and he seemed to polish and care for that thing as if it was family.

In the same year as the great storm, my Grandad passed on. I went up to the Cross by the hill and sat. I guess I started talking to my Grandad – I knew that he'd be listening wherever he was.

It was right then that Woodrow found me. He said we should get down off the hills as it was going to rain heavy. It started just as we got into Woodrow's house.

My big pal went over to that particular box of his, and he seemed to put something in a smaller box, and then he handed that small box to me.

"Take this little one. Please keep it safe. It's a small bit of the magic that I keep in that box over there."

I asked Woodrow what was in it, and all he said was, "It's a little piece of hope. That'll see you through all the bad years. Don't look inside. Never look inside, or else it'll fly away."

You're going to say I'm crazy, but I kept that little box with me all my life. When I was at college, or in a job, or my marriage proposal – and especially at the birth of my child. Every time I needed a little piece of magic, I'd hold that little box tight and wish for the best. It always gave me strength.

When Woodrow finally gave up the ghost, I went back home to the village. His family said that he had left something for me in his Will. It was his big box from the fireplace.

I went up the hill to talk to Woodrow because I knew he'd be listening just like my Grandad, and I'm sure I heard him say that I was to open the magic box. So, I did – and do you know what was in it? Nothing. It was empty. I smiled.

I decided to open the other little box that I had taken with me everywhere – all the years of my life. And do you know what? It was empty too. The gift that Woodrow had given me was plain hope and belief in myself and my life.

No bigger or smaller gift than that. Thank you, Woodrow. Thank you kindly.

THE GREAT CHAOS OF SHOREHAM VILLAGE

That summer, that glorious, glorious summer, sat on the shoulder hills of the little village and warmed the hearts of its inhabitants.

The heat had slowed everything and everyone down to a more comfortable life, more in tune with that of the eighteenth century than today's horrors. This perfectly suited Miss Sligerhorn, the village spinster – a role, by the way, that she had been born to play. No harsh word would leave her mouth regarding the heatwave, not for her the fast and furious lifestyles of some of her racier neighbours; no, Miss Sligerhorn was definitely in her comfort zone.

Each morning at precisely 5.52 am, the Colonel, a strange fruit indeed, would cross Miss Sligerhorn's path, and they would greet each other politely and courteously. Yet, an outsider would probably sense an underlying hostility to the proceedings. There had been talk, and I emphasise that it was only talk, that Miss Sligerhorn had been left at the altar by the Colonel, a most deplorable state of affairs.

Every day, pleasantries met, exchanged, and forgotten, Miss Sligerhorn would continue on her way to the cake shop she inherited from her mother. A mother who deserves a story unto herself, but we will put that excitement aside for another time when the days are shorter, and we can rest by a large fire.

Miss Sligerhorn was the gentlest of all creatures and considered most men to be brutes. The Colonel, on the other hand, was a brute and considered most women to be useless.

They lived in the little village of Shoreham, which had a pub, where the men would congregate and quaff ales, and Miss Sligerhorn's cake shop, where the women would meet to discuss in great detail the men that they had unfortunately married. All of them had entered matrimony with careless haste, and all of them were now regretting their actions at leisure. This had been the way of things since the dawn of time, but things were about to change as we shall see.

In London, Town life was increasingly fraught and was made all the worse by the heightened temperatures. It would be a truth to say that living and working in the city was far from a pleasant experience, especially for the great and good who ran the country.

For several years now, there had been increasing criticism of the politicians who controlled the purse strings, who made the laws and fiddled their expenses. Greed was the order of the day, and such were the financial cutbacks that if one were to be a politician nowadays, it would have to be for the love of the job rather than the benefits.

In those current dog days, love was a rare thing, a scarce thing indeed. Therefore, one bright Friday afternoon, the Prime Minister and the rest of the blameless walked out of Parliament and closed the store, as they say. They shut up shop and refused to return until the people of the land came to their senses and saw what a spectacular job they all had been doing - which was never going to happen if we're being totally honest.

So there we have the situation, a stalemate where neither party is going to back down, causing the world around them to begin sinking into the mire. Some local authorities attempted to collect rubbish, clean the streets and keep the services rattling on even as the money ran out.

"Look, chaps, we're looking for volunteers this weekend to clean the sewerage system. So if you could raise your hands to show interest, that would be truly marvellous; what, no one, no one at all?"

So not only did the heatwave cause the country to revert to eighteenth-century travel, the simmering politics caused the villages and towns to close in on themselves, and each tiny hamlet became judge, jury and council for all of its inhabitants.

Shoreham was no exception, but I guess you knew that. If it had been possible to build a castle keep around this village, they would have done so, but time and money constraints had put paid to that idea.

The good folks of Shoreham didn't want the scoundrels from Otford, their neighbouring village, to come looking for those things that were in short supply in Otford. It was a time for fortitude, for kindness, for mercy, for every village looking after itself and to hang with the rest.

Shoreham consisted of two streets: Church Street and High Street. They were laid out in a letter 'T', meaning there were three entrances to and from the little haven that had to be manned and guarded. The fact that anyone could freely drive through the lanes that crisscrossed the fields did not appear to come into the equation. The defence was more a matter of visibility than practicality, and it was a Maginot line populated by Miss Marples and Colonel Blimps.

The village kids ignored the gates as if they didn't exist, and when the 'Gate Controller' (the Colonel's idea) asked 'Who goes there?' – the kids would just stare at the questioner and continue walking.

This whole indiscipline issue was beginning to annoy the Colonel, so much so that he'd teamed up with Roger Hartness – agreed by all, to be the angriest man in the village. Roger was known to shout at cats that had peed anywhere other than their own gardens. He had photographs in his study of which animals belonged to which property. Roger was married, which came as a shock to most people when they first found out. His wife, Tina, was the gentlest soul in the universe. Perhaps she had to be – two angry people would have been challenging to maintain in the one house.

"Curfew!" that was Roger's summation of the problem. "The oldies are always in bed relatively early, so the only folks to be upset with the curfew would be the youngsters. I propose a village-wide curfew of, say, 9 pm."

To enforce the curfew Roger and 'friends' would patrol the streets after that time and 'encourage' the stragglers to get home as quickly as possible. Naturally, there would be shift workers, but as long as they registered with Ground Control (Roger's idea that one), things would go smoothly or 'tickety boo' as Roger liked to say.

Now, this is where things get a little sticky – the Colonel, Roger and 'friends' controlled the south gate at the bottom of Church Street. Miss Sligerhorn and her posse controlled the High Street and the two exits involved with that road. Since the Colonel suggested a curfew and patrol, you can bet your sweet bippies that Miss Sligerhorn went out of her way to avoid such an action.

There was a de-militarised zone at the junction of the High Street and Church Street, which had to be crossed frequently by the former's drinkers because the pub was in Church Street and therefore under the jurisdiction of the Colonel. The cake shop and tea rooms, on the other hand, sat on the High Street and were under the patronage of Team Sligerhorn.

A meeting had to be set up between the parties, and the Village Hall was proposed. However, it was situated too deep into the Sligerhorn camp to be considered a neutral venue.

Outside the village and on the main city road, a burger van sold coffee, burgers, and onions with fries at very reasonable prices (their slogan). So this was to be the setting for the summit.

Miss Sligerhorn and her followers turned up first and were heard to say 'typical' quite a few times under their breaths, even although they had just passed through the Colonel's territory and saw that his team were still in the stages of getting ready. Thirty minutes later and all in red berets, the Colonel's Church Street gang arrived.

Miss Sligerhorn had done much 'tutting' over the

last half hour, not just because of the lateness of the other lot but also because of the prices the burger van man was charging.

"We're in the middle of the Great Chaos, or hadn't you heard Miss Prim and Proper," said the burger van owner with a hint of disgust.

"And that means you can charge what you like, does it?" Asked an angry Miss Sligerhorn, who turned away from the van without waiting for an answer.

It didn't stop the burger van man shouting after her, "I've got overheads to consider. I've got to go and collect the burgers myself, thanks for asking," but she wasn't asking; she was already drinking tea from a flask she had brought. She then turned to Irene, her Lieutenant, and issued a statement, "Irene, fifteen pence on all our buns. Make a note of it if you please." Irene scribbled the message with a large butcher's pencil and her tongue hanging out.

"Fifteen pence on buns," said a self-satisfied Irene as she hit the notebook with the lead end of her giant pencil.

"And twenty pence on fondant fancies," shouted Miss Sligerhorn, causing Irene to bring out her large butcher's pencil and tongue once again.

When the meeting began, Miss Sligerhorn was the

first to speak. "We are not at war, Colonel," she said, suddenly realising there was a double meaning to her statement.

"Agreed"
"So why the need for a curfew?" asked the lady who he may have jilted at the marriage altar (or not).
"Because we are in the midst of the Great Chaos", shouted the burger van owner, who had heard that phrase from one of the more down-market newspapers.
The Colonel stood up to show off his imposing 6 foot 4 inches of height and demanded a hush from the crowd.

"Dear, dear lady, I am not the power-hungry mad man that your people are putting about the cake shop, I am just a concerned citizen who worries about the youth of this nation, the youth of this country - after all, these people are our future, our investment, as it were," and the Colonel started to hit his palm with his fist as if this was the culmination of a lifetime of struggle until someone shouted, "Sit down you old fart, you're ruining my business." As you may have guessed, it was the burger van man.

A vote was eventually taken, and the Colonel's people voted, not surprisingly, for a curfew, and all the Sligerhorn gang voted against a curfew.

Someone mentioned that the Sligerhorn part of the village was in the posher area and that votes should count double over there, but that lady was told to take a walk by someone from the Colonel's team who also said they would punch her on the nose if she didn't shut up this minute.

So nothing was decided that day, and the village grew, sadly, a little further apart as a result.

On the Church Street side were the village tennis courts, available for hire at subsidised rates. They were now no longer in use, that is until the Colonel came up with an idea.

The courts had a wire mesh surrounding them up to a good height of 12 feet; this allowed the balls to avoid hitting the friendly people of Shoreham. The fence would be hard to scale, and that is why by the following morning, most of the curfew breakers who attempted to enter the village by the Church Street entrance were now being held prisoner in the tennis courts.

"We'll hold them until they've learned their lesson," decreed the Colonel. Standing at each corner on step ladders were men holding buckets full of tennis balls. If any of the curfew breakers had dared to move, one of the men would throw a tennis ball to deter them. However, being British and in charge of a tennis ball meant that not one curfew breaker ever got hit: an unfortunate but actual fact.

The Colonel had attempted to curtail visiting times to deprive the youngsters of family support. Still, it had a limited effect as the families just sat on the hill above the courts throwing chocolate bars and packets of crisps into the 'prison'.

By Saturday, the whole of the village youth, including those who lived in High Street, had been imprisoned. If we are being honest, most of the parents were enjoying the break. They knew where their kids were, that they were being looked after and couldn't get into trouble.

"Let the Colonel sort them out. See how he likes it," was the typical response, and to be honest, the Colonel was at his wit's end.

He had attempted to keep the kids entertained by playing something called a 'record player' and music by people called 'The Beatles' – but none of the kids seemed interested until he threatened to take away their phones and music players if they didn't listen.

A child without a phone is a child ready to start a revolution.

The Colonel sent in his men with berets to take away the kids' phones and pods. Asking them to hand them over hadn't been a huge success, so forced removal seemed the only option. The team was to be led by Angry Roger, who, as it happens, had found himself not to be as angry as the Colonel and was more of a slightly miffed Roger.

As soon as the team entered the compound (the Colonel's description), they were surrounded, stripped naked and tied to the fences. Within fifteen minutes, the kids had walked out of the tennis courts free as the day they were born and still in possession of their phones.

But they didn't stop there, the Colonel was dragged outside his home, and a rope tied around his ankles, then hung upside down from a lamppost.

Even though he kept shouting that the blood was running to his head, no one paid the slightest bit of attention to him. Later in the day, the kids started to play a game where they used the upside-down Colonel to play skittles. Large plastic bottles were stood on end, and the Colonel was swung around to see how many he could knock down. Miss Sligerhorn and her team took on the village teenagers and did themselves proud by winning after a tie break.

The following Monday, the 'Great Chaos' was over

as the politicians had had enough of sitting at home; the Government returned to making laws and fiddling expenses, Miss Sligerhorn had a re-launch of her cake shop but, like the burger van man, refused to reduce her prices to pre-Chaos levels, especially on those fondant fancies.

Without much ado, the world returned to where it had been before, which is in a much bigger mess but with people talking to each other.

By Tuesday of the following week, Miss Sligerhorn and the Colonel were wishing each other a 'good morning' with the usual unspoken reservations at 5.52 am.

All was good and right with the world.

THE FIRST SHOREHAM VILLAGE PLAYERS

To be honest, I'd never actually heard of Gertrude Swansway. She was one of those 'larger-than-life' characters, and to the locals in Shoreham at the end of the 19th century, she was simply known as 'Aunt Gertie'.

Whenever you needed anything organised, arranged, or distributed, Aunt Gertie was your lady. The reason that so much is remembered about her life is the fact that she left so many diaries.

However, there had always been one journal missing, that of the year 1901. This question was answered when the diary turned up several weeks ago under the floorboards of one of the large houses down by the river, currently being renovated. In Gertrude's journal of 1901 was recorded the funeral of Queen Victoria and the opening of the new Co-operative shop on Shoreham High Street. So why did she hide the journal?

Contained within the pages were scribblings to suggest that Aunt Gertie had been a paramour of the new King of England.

We'll leave those stories for another time and get to the critical part of the story.

The year 2024 will be the 100th anniversary of the Shoreham Village Players, but this wasn't the first drama society formed in the village – in her journal, Aunt Gertie discussed how she and Minty Minton and Sasha Dogoody in July 1901 formed the Shoreham Strolling Troubadours.

Minty had mentioned at their inaugural meeting that "Something should be done to cheer the ballyhoo village up. Weren't we now in the modern age, the Edwardian age," at which point Aunt Gertie blushed.

 "I suggest we put on a ballyhoo show," said Minty. Sasha Dogoody said, "As long it does not involve that dwedfull Oscar Wilde". Minty felt that was rather a shame, but Aunt Gertie insisted we should not mention that horrible man's name again. Then Minty came up with a corker – "why don't we put on Three Men in A Boat?" Shasha Dogoody said, "You mean dat spiffing little story by Jerome K Jerome?" "Exactimondo", said Minty and "I know the very ballyhoo place to stage it".

And that, dear friends, is why the first ever recorded drama production in Shoreham was actually held on the river.

Minty had taken charge from the word go. "I see myself as J", said Minty, "you Gertie can be George, and Sasha shall be Harris. Mrs Trafalgar's pooch can play Montmorency. So, it's all settled," ....and apparently it was.

"I see the whole thing taking place upon a little boat in the middle of the Darent river," said Minty getting ever so excited." We shall tie the boat to the bridge, and the audience will bring hampers and sit by the river". Gertie was to write the ballyhoo play, and Sasha could stitch together some marvellous costumes.

Minty suggested holding the rehearsals after dark "to maintain secrecy", and they went ever so well. But many habitants of the village who made their way home from the nearby hostelry believed that they could hear supernatural voices.

One such man, Ebenezer Twislewaite, was so frightened by the experience that he took an oath never to drink again – that was until the day he got hit by a runaway horse and sadly expired.

Then came the big day," the Grande Journee," said Minty in his somewhat over-excited manner. Many of the great and good were sitting in anticipation on either bank of the river. Hampers were opened and oodles of food consumed.

However, dear friends, I have to mention at this juncture – that the evening prior, when the three were having their dress rehearsal in the dark – it had rained very heavy, very heavy indeed.

To say that the river was torrential on the day of the performance was instead to underestimate it.

It was just as Aunt Gertie was shouting (very deep voice), "Montmorency, Montmorency, where are you?" That the tiny boat began to slip its mooring – that is to say, from being tied to the bridge. No one noticed at first, and as the boat edged down the river a little, the picnickers just moved their derrières a few inches further along the bank.

However, when the boat finally did break loose, it was very noticeable since Sasha Dogoody somehow managed to remain tied to the bridge and went flying off the back of the boat – just as Aunt Gertie and Minty started on a rather fateful voyage downstream.

The last they heard of Sasha was as she shouted, "be bwave fellow thespians, be bwave".

Minty shouted to Gertie, "... I do believe that you should also play the part of Harris, Gertie."

(Deep voice) "Why should I?" "Because I don't know the ballyhoo part, that's why", screamed a panicky Minty.

It was also apparent to those ashore that the audience had now broken into a trot and then a run, attempting to follow the boat downstream.

"Gertrude, please speak up and please try to make the voices of George sound different from that of Harris."

Aunt Gertie got ever so cross and warned Minty (deep voice), "I may be a lady, but one more derogatory word about my acting and by God I'll give you a sound thrashing within an inch of your life".

Monty had never heard Auntie Gertie talk like that, and to say Monty was stunned was an understatement – that is until he was actually stunned when the boat hit the second bridge. Unfortunately, Monty was standing and took the full force, ending up face down in the river. Aunt Gertie had fallen back onto the deck and so avoided hitting any large objects.

Nothing could cool Gertie's temper, however, and when Police Constable Wikenshaw of Otford constabulary tried to help her to her feet – his face appeared to stop Aunt Gertie's fist.

That evening, Minty was taken to a hospital in Bromley. Aunt Gertie cooled her heels in Sevenoaks' jail. Everyone forgot about Sasha

Dogoody, who literally hung about the bridge for several hours afterwards.

The following week, the Shoreham Strolling Troubadours was officially closed down by a vote of 3 votes to nil.

Minty suggested they never speak of it again.

And that, dear friends, is the real beginning to the Shoreham Village Players.

Let no one tell you otherwise.

A DIARY FOUND IN THE VILLAGE CHURCH

Friday 9th July

Maybe I should start at the very beginning, then perhaps if someone finds this, it will all make more sense. That is if what has just happened can make sense - to anyone.

I live (lived) in a beautiful village in the southeast of England. I don't want to be any more exact than that, just in case, they find this.

A week ago, we had the village fete, with all its usual sunshine, and games and I remember thinking to myself, what a perfect place to live. Old misery-guts ran the whole show, moaning, as he usually did, about everything. Yet the fete always seemed to take place and, in the end, would always manage to be better than the year before.

The village has several excellent pubs, which took turns to supply the drinks on the day of the fete. There was a stall for strawberries, one selling flowers, another for support of the local drama society and one where Mrs Laud told peoples' fortunes for a small donation to the church.

Oh, yes, and there's a church which you'll see is very important – but I'll get to that.

It's a friendly little place where everyone knows everyone and knows secrets (or say they do) about the rest of the village. I think the village works on the premise that everyone has at least one secret they would rather keep to themselves. If people don't know what it is, the kind folks of the village will make one up. Not much different, I would imagine, from anywhere else in this glorious land.

I think I am going to use this notebook to record two things. The first is to record what is happening right now to the place where I live, and the second is to recall stories about the great, the good and the downright stupid who have lived in the place since I came to stay here – which must be about 25 years ago; time flies.

I discovered it by accident. I just happened to be driving along the high road when I saw a sign for the village and fell in love with the place immediately. It's that type of place – the kind of village you only find once in a lifetime.

The first sign of anything unusual was the 'phones going dead – any and every 'phone, it seemed. Sometimes this happened in a small village. Sometimes it snowed, and we'd be cut off for a day or two. I mean, it's only 20 miles from London, but you can still be isolated down here.

I had gone down to the George pub to see if anyone else had the same problem. Annie told one of her staff to turn on the television to see if there was any news. And guess what? That was only showing a blank screen with the odd spark every so often.

"Maybe some transmitter's down," said Annie in her usual reassuring way.

"What transmitter?" Asked old Jake, who questioned everyone and everything.

"How should I know, Jake? Just sit there and sup your beer," she scolded, which was quickly followed by a smile.

"It's the Russians," scowled Jake. "Probably marched through Ukraine all the way to London, like as not. Or maybe it was them North Koreans. Never trusted them".

The rest of us smiled at Jake, the way we always smiled at Jake.

It was just before seven that someone mentioned they hadn't heard any trains that afternoon, and I quickly realised they were correct. I couldn't recall hearing the London train pass either.

"Maybe someone should ring the church bells, let the village folks know that it's seven o'clock," said Annie.

I mentioned that people could just look at their watches or clocks, but as Jake pointed out, they had all stopped, too.

So, when the rest of them in the pub looked at me, I knew I had been volunteered to go and ring the bells. I had messed about with bell-ringing once upon a time.

I walked into a beautiful summer's evening. The village has no street lighting (although that's common around these parts and won't give a clue as to where we are) – and as I walked up the street, I could see through the windows families sitting down together, maybe for the first time without the television invading their evening meals.

As I crossed the street to go through the church gate, I noticed the last house suddenly go dark inside. At the time, I didn't think much about it until I tried the switches in the church hall, and every one of them failed to work.

I had climbed up to the church tower many times to look at the bells (eight in all) – so accomplishing this in the dark wasn't a hardship.

I pulled my way carefully up the iron-rung ladders and balanced my way across the narrow beam, which took me to a small platform on the other side of the tower. There was only enough room for one man or woman up there. The bells looked okay and standing up, so I thought I'd go down a start ringing down one of them.

That was when I heard the noise. I wasn't sure who or what it was, but it sounded like a train on the rails was in trouble. Then I heard men shouting. Perhaps a train had crashed into a transmitter or something and knocked everything out.

I climbed the last ladder (which took a person up to the very top of the church tower) to have a better look. I don't know what made me hesitate - most probably my fear of heights - but I decided not to stand but look through one of the holes in the brick which let rainwater out.

I remember once when I was making a parachute jump up in Scotland, my brain had decided to take a back seat – it's the only way I can describe it – and it felt as I plummeted to the ground that I was watching a movie, and all this wasn't happening to me.

This was the same feeling. As I looked through the hole in the church tower, I could see tanks – the military sort – followed by soldiers with guns. I could just make out their shouting, and it wasn't any language I had ever heard before.

The village was being invaded. I could see from the tower the same uniformed men coming in from both sides of the High Street.

As the tanks turned the corner into the street below the church, several of the soldiers broke off and ran to the doors of the houses, kicking them in.

I saw the Smith family, who lived in the first cottage, being dragged out and made to kneel in the middle of the road.

That was when I felt my world changed on its axis. The Smith's eldest son got up to challenge one of the soldiers, and another of them shot the boy dead.

I fell back onto the floor of the tower and started to shake. Maybe they were making a television programme? Something I hadn't heard about. When I had pulled myself together a little, I had another look. The rest of the Smiths were being marched at gunpoint down the street. Mrs Smith was forcibly removed from the body of her dead son.

My next thought was that maybe the Smiths were terrorists, but that was cut short when I saw more families being forced onto their knees in the street.

What the hell was happening to my world? This group of people, whoever they were, were rounding up the whole village. I heard some of them kick in the church door below me. There was more shouting in this strange language as they knocked over furniture in the church.

I could hear someone try to climb the iron ladders – they were coming up for me. I made myself as small as possible and pushed my body into the corner of the tower.

It sounded as if one of the soldiers was helping the other up the ladder. I waited on them finding me.

Suddenly the soldier fell from the ladder and must have landed on the other because I could hear them argue – whatever the language was.

This must have deterred them because I saw them run out of the church and back onto the street. I stayed hidden until the sky was pitch black and only the stars above me.

I was desperate for some water and decided that I might try to find something to drink as I hadn't heard anything for a while.

I held my breath and lowered myself down to the middle platform – I put my ear to the floor, but I could hear nothing. I descended into the church, and it was totally black, although I could feel chairs and tables lying upside down.

I knew the bell ringers kept some bottled water at the back of the church and guessing where I was; I crawled towards the rear wall.

I located the cabinet and found three bottles of the stuff. I drank that first bottle in one go, and it was just as I wiped the corner of my mouth that I heard the church door open.

Saturday 10th July

I had slept badly in the church tower, resting my head against one of the larger bells. The young girl, who couldn't have been more than nine or ten, lay hidden in a little cove at the western end of the attic.

Her name was Elise, and she had managed to hide in an outhouse at her home. She had heard her family being dragged out the door by some people she couldn't see.

"I heard my mother call my name, and then my mother shouted, 'coming Elise'," this is what she shouts when we play hide and seek, and she wants me to hide.

"So, I didn't make a sound or move."

Elise had waited for several hours before she made a move. Her home, she said, had been left with furniture and books scattered all over the place. Her father had always told her that if she couldn't find her family, she was to go to the church as she would be safe there. So that is what she had done.

Elise was as mystified as me. We live in what is known as one of the most beautiful spots in the country and possibly the quietest and safest, and yet within a matter of hours, all of that had changed.

She was a brave little soul, perhaps braver than me, and here we were, the two of us lost.

Just after dawn, I heard the sound of a gun being fired in the hills above the village. Normally, I would associate it with a farmer killing some vermin or other – but then the strange thought crossed my mind that it might be the vermin shooting the farmer – whoever the vermin were; I was still unclear who was carrying all this out.

When it became light enough to make out specific landmarks, I managed to get to a position in the church tower which let me see much of the surrounding area - without giving away my presence (I hoped).

Once or twice, I heard small vehicles coming and going on the High Road. I had the thought that perhaps those responsible had considered this part of the village cleared of all people and that maybe they were no longer showing any interest in the church.

I saw a dark figure making their way along Church Street towards me, keeping mainly to the shadows. I also noticed a large gap between the shadows in front of the Old Post Office and those in the car park of the Kings Arms. It meant whoever this was would be seen for an amount of time.

When they ran from the safety of the first building, I saw it was that of a man – known to us as the president of the Parish Council, Thom Drey, whose family had lived in the village for generations.

As he came out into the light, a small, armoured vehicle appeared from nowhere and shot him first in the legs and then in the chest. Some man in a khaki uniform jumped from the vehicle and dragged Thom by one leg - finishing off with throwing his body like an old dog in the back. I assumed from his motionless body that Thom was dead, but as the jeep turned the corner in front of the church, Thom had one last go at upsetting the enemy, and he appeared to try to hit the driver with a wrench. It was the last thing he did – I don't want to go into too much detail here except to say it wasn't a pretty death.

I must have made quite a noise because it brought Elise up to the roof, and she could see I was upset. I tried to stop her from looking over the tower, but it was in vain, and when she saw what had happened to Mr Drey, she let out a piercing scream. He had been her godfather.

As I pulled her down from view, I saw enough to know that the two soldiers had stopped what they were doing and were indeed heading towards the church.

What the hell was I going to do? I was trying to look after myself, but I had a young girl to protect as well. Leastways, that was how I had read the situation - but how wrong can one desperate person be?

SHOREHAM, CHRISTMAS, 1958

They had called her Elizabeth, after the Queen since she had unexpectedly turned up on the Coronation day.

Now Elizabeth considered herself a grown-up, having turned six years of age a few months earlier. She was packed to the brim with the life force itself, and God couldn't have pushed any more into this particular package. She was a tornado.

If tall monsters existed back then, then they were well hidden. Children had the run of the village, in those days, from sun-up to sun-down. They were fed in the morning, and then they disappeared until their names were called as the sun started to sink behind the Cross.

That was life back then, sunshine and playtime, endless days and changing friendships.

Elizabeth was a curious child, which was just a polite way of saying that she was a nosey kid. She would sometimes sit across from the church, or village hall, or even one of the public houses and watch and listen. She never told anyone about anything she found out, just that she kept it all to herself, knowing that one day she was going to write a book about it all (and probably spend a lot of time in court).

Elizabeth lived in one of those bijou cottages, which nestled comfortably across from the Old George Inn; a pub, like all of the six pubs in the village – which had its time in the sun, followed by months or years of quiet reflection, but the good times always came back to each of them. New lives, new worlds, regenerations.

Young Elizabeth lived with her two maiden great-aunts, Jenny and Nancy, on account of her parents going down to a tube station during a gas leak and both never seeing daylight again.

For the most part, she was a happy little child, one who found so much love in the world that she had a lot to give to others.

One night, in the winter of 1958, Elizabeth was playing out in the little courtyard at the rear of Church Cottages. From the window above, she could hear her Aunt Nancy crying.

"There, there, don't weep so," said Aunt Jenny.

"My heart is broken, Jenny. Split into two sorrowful parts," said Aunt Nancy, who had probably read too many Bronte novels.

Elizabeth had heard all this crying and seen all these tears before. Her Aunt Nancy's fiancé had gone off to war and never returned. The story was not that he had met some glorious death on the battlefield but that he had taken up with a barmaid who worked in a small hotel just outside of Paris. Apparently, they had three very healthy children and a wonderful life; Nancy refused to believe it.

"She kidnapped him, I know it," she cried. "I will die of a broken heart. Mark my words, Jenny. You see, if I don't." Sometimes during these sorrows, Aunt Nancy would take an attack of the vapours.

Elizabeth had not known what to make of it all when she was four years old, or at five, but now that she was six and a woman, it was time she did something about it.

Elizabeth decided to walk up to the village shop on Church Street, and in there, she asked if they sold anything for a broken heart.

"Oh bless, Elizabeth, you are too young for a broken heart," said the posh little lady who served her, the one who smelled of moth-balls.

"It's not for me. It's for my Aunt Nancy, silly."

The woman in the shop nudged the other woman, and both knew precisely what this meant – Nancy was in one of her Miss Havisham periods. She usually had a 'jilted-bride' season every year (especially if the weather was less than kind).

The shop-woman jokingly offered Elizabeth a needle and thread and looked at the little girl with a 'that's the best I can do' expression. Elizabeth said, 'no, thank you' and walked up to the High Street.

It suddenly hit her that the butchers at the corner of Crown Road might be a place to try; after all, they had hearts going spare.

"How can I help you?" Asked the butcher.

Elizabeth told him that her Aunt needed something to fix a broken heart and that maybe he would have one he didn't want.

The butcher smiled and explained that even if he did have a spare heart, it probably wouldn't do her Aunt any good.

"Everyone knows that your Aunt Nancy has the biggest heart in the village. Nothing I have could give you could replace the beautiful heart that she already has."

Disappointed, Elizabeth decided to head back to Church Street. As she approached the Village Hall, she met her friend, Rose, and Rose's mother. They were heading to see Santa, who had left his sleigh at the rear of the Hall (everyone knew that in Shoreham). Elizabeth had forgotten that Santa was coming to the village. Usually, her Aunts would take her to see him, but they all had forgotten what with all the crying and such.

"Why don't you come with us?" Said Rose's mother.

And that is what she did. Of course, you can guess what she asked Santa to bring her at Christmas: a new heart for her Aunt.

Santa laughed and chuckled and then smiled at the little girl.

"That is a kind thing to ask for," said Santa. "It would mean you wouldn't have anything for yourself."

Elizabeth said that she would rather her Aunt was happy than she had a present from Santa.

"You are kindness, itself," said Santa. "I'll tell you what I'll do, I will bring you a present of your choosing on Christmas Eve, and I will give you a letter to take to your Aunt."

"Will it mend her broken heart?" Asked Elizabeth.

"I can't see it doing any harm," said Santa.

Elizabeth and Santa shook on it, and then she told Santa what she would like for Christmas, and Santa said it would be in her stocking on Christmas Day when she awoke.

Santa left for a few minutes and returned with a letter addressed to 'The Wonderful Aunt Nancy'.

On Christmas morning, Nancy took herself off to the bedroom and decided to open the letter Santa had given her.

"Dear Nancy,

Your little niece has told me, with the utmost concern, that you might die of a broken heart one day soon. I realise that you are too old to sit on Santa's knee, but if you could, this is what I would tell you. Live your life, Nancy. Live it with so much optimism and enthusiasm that you will almost burst at the seams. Nothing can break happiness. Life will be good for you again. I am Santa. I know what I am talking about. Smile even although the light at the end of the tunnel may be a train coming the other way. If you were a Christian in the Coliseum, I would have told you to do the same. With the Lions staring at you – you smile. Life, in the end, will defeat us, even Santa, but if you have so much love and life in your heart, then you can go out on your terms. You will love again, Nancy. Believe me—beat life at its own game. Be happy.

Merry Christmas, Santa Claus."

Elizabeth's Aunt Nancy came back downstairs, smiling so broad that it looked as if her head might fall off.

"I think I'll have that sherry now," she said, and then she winked at her much-loved niece, who was having the best Christmas ever.

TOMMY AND I CYCLE TO SHOREHAM - 1901

Whenever Tommy was excited or stressed, which, to be honest, was most days, he'd put the word 'chuffing' in front of everything. For instance, today was going to be a blooming chuffing day with loads of chuffing hills to cycle up, and when we got to the ballyhoo top, well, we'd chuffing have a pick nick.

Do you see what I mean?

Tommy was a good egg, a decent sort who would lift a finger to help anyone, a talented tennis player, cyclist, and an excellent footballer. On the other side, he was a frightful drunk, which, thank goodness, had only been that once. He was also highly competitive – and would bet you a farthing on who would blink first. Apart from that, he was the kind of gent you would be proud to call a friend.

So come Saturday morning, Tommy and I would be on our chuffing bicycles, out of the chuffing city and heading for the chuffing countryside (I promise to limit the use of chuffing in future), and this Saturday was no exception.

Tommy knocked at my door at 5.30 (in the morning, may I say – I didn't even know there was a 5.30 in the morning if truth be told). "Get up, you chuffing wastrel" was the morning cry of the

Tommesara Smitheratist bird, and it tended to awaken everyone else up as well.

"Will you please tell that foolish friend of yours that it is far too early in the morning for his buffoonery," said my rather grumpy Father without opening his eyes (apparently, it helped him get back to sleep quicker). Like Tommy, my father tended to hook in a word and then beat it to death with its overuse. 'Buffoon' and 'buffoonery' were both in the process of getting six shades of purple knocked out of them. Luckily, he hadn't heard Tommy's current obsession, or that would have resulted in me having to leave home and declaring myself an orphan.

"Apologies, Holmes, but we have the whole of the southeast to explore, and time is chuffing moving on."

Ever since he'd read The Adventures of Sherlock Holmes, I had received that name. It was better just to smile and accept my fate because he might come up with something far, far worse. Tommy wanted to be known as Moriarty on our cycling trips because he said the name felt good on his tongue. I know what you're thinking; Tommy wasn't the most intelligent of my friends.

By six o'clock in the morning, we were happily cycling over the Thames and heading down the Old

Kent Road where the world was waiting to
entertain Holmes and Moriarty.

"First stop, chuffing breakers," said my pal.
For those that don't speak Tommyese, that meant
breakfast must be had with all haste.

Toast, crumpets, and coffee were the order of the
day at Mrs O'Reilly's tearoom in Lewisham, a
bargain at one shilling. Mrs O'Reilly had long since
departed this life and gone to the great tearoom in
the sky. The place was run by a man with the name
of Derek.

"'Mrs. O'Reilly's' sounds that bit more romantic,"
said a very tattooed Derek. "People knows what to
expect, with that name, but Derek's Cafe, well it
just doesn't sound right, do it?"

Both I and Tommy left the premises, agreeing that
Derek was correct in what he had said but that we
should avoid the place in future as Derek seemed
to be two seagulls short of an aviary.

Although it had been five months, Tommy still
insisted that he wear a black band on his right arm
as a mark of respect for the old Queen. I told him
that this was a new and exciting time, that this was
a new century, this was 1901, after all, and
goodness knows what the next hundred years
would bring.

Tommy felt that the new century could chuffing well wait until his mourning was chuffing done. I know I promised to keep the use of 'chuffing' to a minimum, but it seems impossible when in the company of Tommy Smithers, I will try harder – I promise.

Just as we left Bromley, Tommy declared that the countryside had properly started, and although I tried very hard to see it, I was at a loss to notice the difference. Still, Tommy knows what he's talking about, or so he tells me.

After a mile or so, I hinted that perhaps an ale might be the order of the day. Tommy stopped so fast that I almost ran into the back of him.
"I have a plan," he said (actually, he said 'a chuffing plan', but I thought I would spare you that nonsense).
"And your plan is what, Tommy?" that was my contribution to the discussion.
"I know of a little village in the Darenth Valley where the ale is like nectar." Tommy was tasting the ale in his mind's eye.

"Why haven't you told me of this place before?" I ask.
"Because, my dear friend, it is not a place for the unwary."
"Why is that, Tommy?" I ask.

"Because my fine fellow, it is a hotbed of liberalism and creativity. People have really let things slide in this village. Some women are so close to looking like men that one might wish them 'a good morning sir' without realising."
"Well, I never." I declared.

"Worse still.." Tommy looks around before whispering, "..there are men in this village who do not like the company of women. There I've said the chuffing thing. It's too late, but it's out in the big world for all to know."
"Don't like the company of women?" I think I may have looked perplexed.
"You know what I mean, stop being a chuffing idiot. They don't like women."

So I had to have my say, and I mentioned, "I don't know any men who don't like women apart from my Father, who hasn't spoken to my Mother since she tried to fry the porridge. That must be eleven years ago, now."
"Your mother tried to fry porridge?" says Tommy.
"She did, and my Father said that any woman who was stupid enough to try and fry porridge shouldn't expect any conversation to be thrown her way in future, and that was that. He never said a bally word to her again. He said she was an imbecile, a harsh word I grant you, but I think that was his word of the week at that particular time."

I expected Tommy to be impressed with this story, but instead, he said that I should stop talking, chuffing rot and stop acting like an imbecile.

That is why, by the time we got to the little village, Tommy had dropped the word 'chuffing' in favour of the word 'imbecile'. Why hadn't I said that my father had called my mother 'lovable' or had given her money to shut her up? Maybe then Tommy would have done the same.
"Hey, ho, oft we go", shouted Tommy, adding, "you imbecile."

I do rather make things difficult for myself when I don't bally mean to.

The village clock was striking one o'clock as we freewheeled our way down the hill into the centre of this dastardly liberal little village. I had to be honest with Tommy and tell him that I thought the people looked jolly normal.
"Nonsense, you imbecile", was his reply.
We parked up outside a delightful little public house called The Crown. The door was at an angle to the building and led into a small bar for gentlemen.
"Just in case this pub is overrun by liberals, let me do the talking," said reliable Tommy, "just to be on the safe side."

Now to me, the person serving behind the bar was

clearly a man, but Tommy insisted on calling him 'Mam', then winking to me in a pronounced manner, followed by him touching the side of his nose with his finger.

"I didn't want to drink in the place anyway," said a somewhat surprised Tommy, "the establishment looked completely unsavoury. We are well shot of it." At least the barman only asked me to leave, whereas he caught Tommy by the collar and threw him out of the door.

Tommy said that he was right about the place all along, it was a den of liberal-minded imbeciles, and he would be writing to his Member of Parliament just as soon as he returned from the country.

We tried to gain access at the next pub, the Two Brewers, but apparently, Tommy had been there before and was no longer welcome. I didn't realise that you could use so many cursing words in one sentence, but the Two Brewers manager must have broken a record.
"Another den of imbeciles?" I asked.
"Just so."

That is why we came to be sitting outside the Kings Arms drinking two of the most wonderful glasses of ale. This was not, indeed, a den of imbeciles and the prices were exceedingly fair.
Having slaked our thirst, we mounted our trusted

bicycles and headed towards the large town that sat at the hill's top, above the village.

About one-third of the way up the hill, Tommy suggested that we dismount and push our bicycles up the rest of the way. It appears that it didn't do the bicycles much good to be treated to a hill when riding them. To be honest, I thought maybe Tommy found the hill a little too steep, but in fear of being called an imbecile, I refrained.

The climb was worth the effort, and the view over the North Downs was spellbinding.

Why people steal bicycles is beyond me, and two of them at the same time. You have to ask yourself - was the thief a member of some circus troupe? However, the dastardly deed was done, and it meant that cycling back to London was now out of the question. A train was called for, and a train it would be.

Tommy suggested that we travel back by First Class and that I should foot the bill seeing as I was the last one to see the bally bicycles. I think the last time I saw them. I said, "Tommy, do you think the bicycles are safe by that public house?" After which, Tommy called me an imbecile and told me in no uncertain terms that if I was worried about people stealing our property, well, that sort of thing just didn't happen in the countryside. Then he said, "Grow up, man." The next time I looked, the bicycles were gone.

On the way back to the city, a rather plump man and his rather plump wife were playing cards in the railway carriage. The husband appeared to have won the game given that he let out the most frightening cry of 'Ballyhoo'.

I could see the glimmer in Tommy's eyes as he tried the word 'Ballyhoo' out on his tongue.

The word was not found wanting.
Unfortunately.

ONE DAY YOU WILL EVEN MAKE THE ONIONS CRY.

There is a village in the South East of England; perhaps it's yours, maybe it's mine. Perhaps it's a tiny hamlet with a Cross on the hill above it. Who knows?

Sarah hadn't set out to be a writer; in fact, she found that she had difficulty reading when she was at the village school. Everyone else seemed to understand the words, but not her.

Probably later in life, she would find out that she had some minor mix-up in her head, which stopped her fully understanding the way words behaved. She didn't see what others saw but then again, didn't we all?

So, she started to write down the words, one at a time and traced them out with a pencil. She got to know their shapes and meanings. Soon she was putting two words together, and finally, she was writing whole sentences.

By the time Sarah was twelve summers old, she had become a gifted writer, a very gifted writer indeed.

She wrote little essays in school, which she would proudly read out to the class. To be honest, even her teacher smiled in admiration. By the time she was twenty-two, she was writing for a newspaper in the big town next to the village, and she loved her job.

One day in the autumn of 1939, her editor took them all into his little office, offered them cups of tea and then mentioned that there was a war coming.

"It will be our job to keep the people informed. It will be our job to tell the people what they need to know and to keep their morale high."
And that is what they did.

In this little village, of which I speak, which may or may not have a Cross above it on the hill, hard times hit. This little group of houses lay right under the path of the bombers flying overhead. So much so that it would later be known as the most bombed village in that area.

Every single building was wounded in some way, as was every single heart.

The folks at the newspaper kept their promise of telling the people the stories and keeping their morale high, but there was a limit. The government man who visited their offices from time to time would instruct the editor on what could and what couldn't be printed.

So, one evening, Sarah hatched a plan. She started to write little stories of the village and how it had been before the war. They would include some real characters and some that she had made up in her head but had wished that they had lived in her hamlet.

These were little stories that brought smiles to peoples' faces, or perhaps a tear in laughter or one in sadness and with the help of her editor, she managed to print off enough sheets to put one through every letterbox in the streets around her house.

At one end of the High Street lived an older woman who inhabited a big house with empty rooms. No one came to visit, and her only contact with the outside world was Sarah's little weekly stories.

One summer's evening, the old woman lay in wait, and as Sarah came up the path, she opened her door.

Admittedly it startled Sarah at first, but the woman invited her in for a cup of tea. She sat Sarah down and told her that her writing should never stop, unlike the war in the city over the hill.

Sarah smiled, and then the older woman said something that stayed with Sarah for the rest of her years.:

"One day, probably when I am long gone, you will be a great writer, and you will make even the onions cry."

Sarah leaned over and kissed the old lady on her head.
"Thank you," said Sarah.

When Sarah eventually wrote her book after the war, about writing her little stories in a village in the south-east – a village which may or may not have a Cross on the hill above it – she dedicated the book to the woman and what do you think was the title of her book?

'One Day You Will Even Make the Onions Cry'.

A WEEKEND IN SHOREHAM, SEPTEMBER 1939

He looked at the little calendar that his young sister, Emily, had made at school. She had written the 9 of 39 backwards at the top of the sheet. She hadn't even spelt September correctly – but against September 2nd was a reminder that her big brother, Robbie, was in the final night of the play at the village hall.

He had hated the whole process at first, having to stand up in front of folks and say things. Learning the lines was even worse, and it wasn't just Robbie who forgot them. When someone else dried up, the rest of them tended to make it up as they went along – although he did remember his father in Midsummer Night's Dream saying the word 'bumface', which he was sure Shakespeare hadn't written.

And now it was the final night of whatever play it was that he was in. He'd fancied himself as the dashing male lead, but that part had gone to Archie Conway, just like all the girls – Archie could have his pick of any of them.

Robbie had thought that maybe standing up in the village hall would have made him a bit more noticeable to the female population but, so far, it hadn't happened.

He was going to be 18 next week, and he couldn't wait. He and his father were going to go to a football game and then maybe have a beer.

Robbie got very nervous just before he was due to go on stage – not that he had that many lines to say, but he was on the stage a lot of the time.

If he grew bored, he would just look out at the audience, and last night he had seen the vicar sleeping on the front row. On Thursday night, he had seen Tommy and his girlfriend kissing in the back row until Tommy's mother slapped him on the back of the head. Robbie let out a little laugh that didn't really fit in with the play, but no one paid that much attention anyway.

Well, not except Archie's family and all the young girls in the audience who seemed to Robbie to be swooning every time Archie said something.

Some folks get life too easy, thought Robbie. Just then, he noticed everyone looking at him and realised it was his line. What was it again? Was this the long speech or the short one?
He decided it was the short one and said, 'sure thing, Elsie'.

The rest of the cast looked pleased and carried on, so he must have got the right part of the play.

Although on the opening night, he said 'sure thing, Elsie' to Roderick, who was playing an army Captain, which had caused a bit of a titter in the hall.

This acting life wasn't that easy as far as Robbie was concerned, but he still had a passing fancy that he might become a matinée idol of the silver screen – assuming this war thing all died down.

It had been the talk all week with the cast – 'what if we go to war with Germany', 'what if the Germans invade Kent'. Archie Conway yelled out loud that he'd just bang the Krauts on the nose and show them who's boss. All the girls in the room started to swoon. Robbie stuck his fingers down his throat as if he was going to be sick, which caused a few of the men in the room to smile.

Like a family, this village was a wonderful, safe place to grow up. What would happen if the Germans turned up? Okay, so everyone lived on top of everyone else, which sometimes caused friction but didn't happen in all families? And that's precisely what this village was, a family.

The final night of the play went exceptionally well. Robbie thought that maybe folks were having one last night of fun and forgetting their troubles before......well before whatever was going to happen. Robbie wasn't exactly sure what.

They took their curtain call, and the audience stood up and applauded (they hadn't done that on the other nights). Robbie could see the vicar was there again, but this time he wasn't asleep.

As much as he had hated all this acting stuff, he was sure he was going to miss it all. That was why folks acted in these plays in village halls. It brought people together and allowed kids (like Archie) to show off and make people swoon.

Miss Trebor, who had directed and produced the play, clapped her hands for attention and reminded everyone that they were to come to the hall and help clean up after church.

Robbie whistled all the way to the village hall on Sunday. One girl, Jenny, had asked him for his autograph after the performance. He couldn't sleep that night thinking about it.

They all met in the hall at 11.00 am the following day, September 3rd, and Robbie was given the task of sweeping up. A short time later, Miss Trebor came rushing in and told everyone to hush as she switched on the radio. She informed everyone that it was the Prime Minister and we all had to listen:

"This morning, the British Ambassador in Berlin handed the German Government a final Note stating that, unless we heard from them by 11 o'clock that they were prepared at once to withdraw their troops from Poland, a state of war would exist between us.

I have to tell you now that no such undertaking has been received and that consequently, this country is at war with Germany."

Robbie looked over at Archie, who was comforting his sobbing mother. It was going to take more than a punch on the nose to fix this, thought Robbie.

ONCE UPON A SHOREHAM VILLAGE FETE

It happens, it happens to everyone, doesn't it?

You tell a little white lie, and it blows out of all proportions. It runs away and starts a life of its own. It gains a wide circle of friends (more than you have yourself), and then the lie grows so gigantic that it sends you a postcard from somewhere.

Think I'm exaggerating? Okay, maybe a little. See there I go again, lying. Perhaps in your favour, you would have to say that it was done for the best of all reasons – trying to cheer people up.

If Alison hadn't been ill that day, or at least if she hadn't been recovering from a night out in the village, then Jane wouldn't have had to take Alison's place; so, if anyone were to blame, it was Alison and her obvious drink problem. Okay, that's another lie. Alison doesn't have a drinking problem. She had only been at the Mount to taste the wines and had forgotten to stop. But the result was the same, Alison was lying in her bed promising the universe that she had drunk wine for the very, very last time in her life and that not only was she going tee-total, but she would attend church regularly and help the people of Africa – if the universe would only stop her blinking head from hurting as much as it did.

All that was beside the point, for it meant that Jane was now required to fill her best friend's shoes.

When she had agreed to help at the Fete meeting all those months ago, it hadn't seemed like a possibility, and so Jane was happy to nod her head when they asked for a deputy for Alison. It made them sound like a couple of cowboys.

The Shoreham Village Fete was full of all the usual bits and pieces; music, vintage cars, a bar, a tearoom (run by the children and their mums) and the always present ne'er-do-wells, who turned up once a year to promenade around the school ground.

To save money, in this time of austerity, the Fete committee had decided to find the big central acts for the day (those who inhabited the centre-ground – literally) within the immense and obvious talent of the village itself. How hard could it be to procure an act of such breath-taking ability that the village would be talking about it for weeks (or maybe just on Monday morning)?

It was Elsa Fairweather who had opened the bid by telling the committee that she had once been a ballerina (the truth was that she'd spontaneously broken into dance during the Christmas play at school when she was acting as the third shepherd – she had got fed up pointing at the Star and decided that shepherds might dance in times of boredom). She was now twenty-seven years of age and hadn't done anything so physical for the last twenty years.

Elsa was one of those ladies who tended to get up everyone's nose – it wasn't what she did, or said, or in the way she acted – she just annoyed people.

Every village has at least one Elsa – it is the rule. Elsa wasn't a bad person. Instead, she was just someone who had got off the bus at the wrong stop.

Not to be outdone by her nemesis, Alison had said that she could tap-dance – when Elsa remarked that so could she – Alison had upped the stakes by adding that what she had meant to say was that she could tap-dance while standing at the top of a ladder. Elsa took a little time to recoup and then opened with another bid by saying that she could stand on her hands at the top of the ladder while singing the National Anthem.

Jane was sure she could hear Alison swearing under her breath – but there wasn't enough time to ask her, for, by then, Alison had told the committee that she could sing all the songs from Oklahoma while tight-rope walking across the sport's field.

Alison definitely heard Elsa say an extremely rude word out loud, and one or two of the Fete committee also heard her. Mr Grove's face went a very tomato red as he fiddled with his cardigan buttons.

Elsa's husband gave his wife one of those 'here we go again' looks and nodded to her to go to the back of the hall. Elsa and her long-suffering husband huddled together in the corner, and it was difficult for Alison to hear what they were saying.

That was when Alison came up with a rather neat plan – every few seconds, she coughed, and when she did that, she used the noise to cover the rocking of her chair back a little. Although Alison thought she was being subtle, she had moved her chair back several feet (after a few coughs) and was heading towards Elsa – her less-than-subtle plan being evident to most of those in the hall.

Nevertheless, the plan worked, and Alison was sure she heard Derek (Elsa's husband) say, 'you cannot be serious. You know you can't sky-dive'.

After a few minutes (which just gave Alison enough time to stand up and move her seat – less subtly – back to where it had been initially), Elsa reluctantly gave up and said that Alison should sing the songs from the musical while walking a tight-rope. The head of the committee had asked if Alison had an understudy, and Alison had grabbed Jane's arm and shoved it up in the air. Jane wondered what harm could it possibly do?

So, when Jane got the phone call on the Saturday morning of the Fete – it was Mrs Bacchus, the stern one who always smelled of mothballs – who had told Jane that Alison was incapacitated (some old illness she had caught on a gap-year in India, apparently) and that Jane (as her understudy) would have to take Alison's place.

And that is why, on that sunny morning, Jane was dressed in her mother's old tutu with a tartan umbrella for balance and getting ready to walk a tightrope (literally and metaphorically) at the Shoreham Village Fete.

Jane saw two things as she started the death-defying feat. When I say death-defying, Alison had originally said she would walk the rope at 20 feet above the ground (she had actually said five feet but after much tutting from Elsa, Alison had ended up agreeing to that neck-breaking height). When Jane (in her tutu) started crying, the committee kept lowering the rope until it was just two feet high. Still high enough to twist an ankle was how Jane had sold it to them.

So, with all the great and good, and ne'er-do-wells from Shoreham Village watching, Jane managed to move several feet along the rope while singing a Bay City Rollers' song (she didn't know too many proper songs – she had thought of singing 'Wind Beneath My Wings' – until the nerves, she was suffering from, had given her that very problem).

While standing aloft, the other thing she saw was Alison at the back of the crowd (in her sunglasses) smiling. She even had the cheek to wave and stick her thumbs up.

To add insult to injury, Alison mouthed the words 'good luck'. Jane was just about to mouth a very rude word back to her when little Barry Smith twanged the rope she was standing on – causing her to suddenly fly across the bales of hay and straight into the bar, ending up with half a packet of Chorizo flavoured crisps up her nose.

There was spontaneous applause from the whole field.

The committee has asked Jane if she can repeat her act next year. Elsa is learning to sky-dive.

JIMI AND THE PARAKEETS

She knew he wasn't to blame for the birds. At least, not in the other areas of Britain, but here, in Shoreham Village, maybe – just maybe.

She'd met him through Peter, a road manager for the group Pink Floyd who had lived in the village. His daughter, Naomi, born in Shoreham, went on to be a famous actress, but her dad brought the guitarist down to Shoreham to see what an English country village looked like.

Peter and the man had been sitting outside the George pub, in what she could overhear as arguments about music. The man that Peter, referred to as, Jimi was very exotic for this part of Kent, even in the 1960s.

She lived across the street from the pub, in Church Cottages, and would sometimes lie in her room with the window open listening to the lives of folks relaxing at the bar. She knew Peter well and so had followed the two men up to the Cross (at a distance). When they got to the top of the hill, Jimi brought out a cigarette that smelled strange and began to smoke it. Peter told him he didn't smoke.

Jimi must have said something funny because she remembers laughing – although she hadn't intended to.

"Who's there?" Shouted Jimi.

She popped her head over the hedge and smiled.
"Come sit," he said in his American accent.

Peter smiled too and said the three of us should sit
and look at the beautiful village below. Jimi asked if
I played the guitar or any musical instrument, and I
told him I didn't.
"What do you do then, kid?"

That's what he called me, 'kid'.
I told him I was saving up to buy a budgie.
"You like birds?".

I nodded. I spent another hour with them. Then I
told Jimi and Peter I had to be back to eat with my
family. Jimi said he enjoyed our talk, and I've got to
be honest, so did I.

A week or so later, a delivery was made to my
house by Peter. It was two parakeets in a beautiful
cage. The card said: 'They ain't budgies, but they're
just as pretty – Jimi'.

I saw a photo of him in the News of the World, and
I realised his name was Jimi Hendrix.

On the 18th of September, 1970, they announced
that Jimi had died in Notting Hill, London.

I let the parakeets go that day. I released them to be with Jimi. The birds are still here. They are still flying around the village – scores of them.

And as I watch them squawking in the sky, I'll never forget my friend, Jimi Hendrix.

THE LAST SHOREHAM CHRISTMAS

He was 83 when he finally returned to Shoreham.

His daughter had asked what he had wanted for his birthday, a party at his old folks' home? A night out in Toronto?
"No, thank you. I want to go home. See it for one last time."

She understood, and although it would be a long flight if that's what her father wanted, then that was what he would have.

It was nearly Christmas, and as she drove into Station Road, she could see the tears forming in his eyes. There was a giant Christmas tree outside the George, and some folks were laughing and hugging each other - perhaps they had just arrived, or maybe they were just departing.
"I don't suppose they live there anymore - the family."
"I don't suppose they do, Dad."
"They ran that pub for years and years."
"I remember," said his daughter. "I was friends with their children."

They pulled in by the War memorial at the river's edge.
"My father, your grandfather's name is on there."

She turned the car engine off, and the two of them sat in the dark by the Darent. In the distance, she could see some warm Christmas lights coming from a pub beyond the hedge.

"What is that pub called, over there, Dad?"
"That's the Kings' Arms, where I met your Mum for the first time. I remember there was a big log fire that night. I drank several whiskies before your Mum arrived."

"Don't you want to come back in the morning when you can see the village better?" She asked.
"See what better? How it looks now? No thank you. My mind remembers it all as it was, and that's the only village I want to see."
"You could have done that back in Canada and saved yourself a trip."
"No, I had to come here. Just to be here."
"You always loved Christmas here, Dad. Didn't you?"

"Ahh, Christmas in Shoreham. The shops, the tearooms, the Co-operative. The smells and the decorations. One Christmas, I remember well. It was special. Very special, and I had a hand in it."
"You've never told me this one, Dad."
"I'd forgotten, to be honest, at least until now. It came back when I saw all this again."

"So?" He had got her curious. Typically, his stories had been told a thousandfold, and she'd laugh and gasp at the right points, every time.

"Those cottages, I pointed to as we passed the George," said her father.

"Where you used to live?"

"I lived in number one. In those days, the attic ran from one end of the building to the other. You could – if you felt that way inclined – drop yourself into anyone else's house."

"You mean, break-in?"

"In a manner of speaking. Anyway, number three was a bit more modern than our place, and it had a cellar. The people who lived in that cottage were never there, so I used to drop in and search the place."

"You were a thief."

"Never. I never took a thing. I was a boy who had found a den, one that no one else knew about. At least, I thought that was the story. In the cellar of number 3 was a Well. I used to throw old coins down it and make wishes."

"Did any of them come true?"

"I met your Mum, didn't I. One snowy night there was a big hoo-haa – it seemed that some girl from Kemsing had disappeared, just before Christmas and all. The local bobbies were out searching the woods above and below the village. They searched everywhere. At least they thought they had. Many of the folks from the village helped too. When I heard one of the family from the George mention that the girl used to visit her grandmother in number three a long time before.

So I thought it was worth a try. Number three was in darkness, and I thought it safe enough to do my usual..."

"Break into someone's house, you mean?"
"I wish you wouldn't keep saying that. I was just a boy with a strong, curious streak. I went up into the attic and climbed into number three. The place seemed deserted, but I decided to search the cellar. You never know."
"And?"
"I'm getting to it. She was there—the girl from Kemsing. I think I scared her. In fact, I know I did. Once I got her trust, she started to cry. It seemed she was ready to become a mother herself. She's been hiding the fact she was pregnant from her family?"

"How did she get in? Surely she didn't climb the attic?"
"She still had a key. It seems they hadn't changed the lock since her Gran's time. The girl, Rosie, started to moan and said that her tummy hurt. I was scared myself. I don't mind telling you."
"And?"

"I had to let someone know. I ran to the George and told the barman. He came running across. When I returned, the baby was starting to arrive, as it were. John, the barman, ran back and phoned for an ambulance, but the baby was already born by the time they had arrived. It was a boy. The poor little girl wasn't that old herself. She asked me what I should call him, and I suggested George, after the pub. But then she asked what my name was, and I told her, Michael. That was the name she decided on. His name was to be Michael Banks."

"Why didn't you ever tell me this, Dad?"
"I guess it was something I wanted to keep to myself. Something special."

[That was the last time my father ever saw Shoreham. That was his final Christmas. The next day we walked by the river and had lunch in one of the pubs. When my father died, I brought his ashes back to Shoreham to scatter up by the Cross. A few of us had a drink in the Kings Arms afterwards, and an elderly gent was sitting at the next table.

"I am so sorry to hear about your father. Was he from Shoreham? Sorry, I should introduce myself, I'm Michael, Michael Banks."]

CHARLES DICKENS AND SHOREHAM

"But in the world where there is no stay but the hope of a better (world), and no reliance but on the mercy and goodness of God. Through these two harbours of a shipwrecked heart...."

Charles Dickens, letter, October 1865.

I want you to sit comfortably and find comfort in this strangest of tales. Some swear it is true, although there are just as many who would disagree. Perhaps in the passing of the years and in the re-telling, the shadowy remembrance of the truth has been lost. I am hoping, however, that you will be my judge and jury.

Our story concerns one warm day in June 1865 in the most beautiful Kent village of Shoreham, a day like many others where the occupants of this little haven are wrapped up in their day-to-day chores, all of them unaware of a train crash that has taken place several miles away.

The centre of our tale is the Crown public house occupied by the hard-working Mistress Squib and her family.

Eliza Squib has not seen her husband for many a year, but we will not speak unkindly of that soul. Instead, we meet with Eliza as she takes the first opportunity of the day to sit and mend the clothes of her two children.

Her son, who stands beside her, is Obadiah Squib, the man of the house and full of all the life that God can give a heart. His wish is to sail the oceans and, by this method, find his father – but we shall leave that tale for another time.

The boy who sits reading in the corner is the other apple of Eliza's eye, young Benedict, who has been on this earth the merest of summers, yet he is assuming all the finer qualities that could be wished for in a son.

Finally, we meet Charlotte Squib and let no harsh construct be heard against her. Charlotte is a good soul of infinite compassion and has sacrificed her life to work from morn' through late evenings to compensate for her brother's mysterious disappearance, Eliza's errant husband. Ever since her brother's parting, Charlotte has been compelled to repeat the same incantation:

"He will return, I swear it."

Eliza smiles as she has done a thousand times before, and for all their worries and concerns, they are a happy band, and one that providence has decreed should assist our Mister Charles Dickens in his most troubled of times.

And so, our story begins with an innocent knock at the door of the public house.

"Sweet bird of youth and such a time as this; tut, tut"

At the door stands Mister Dickens, his mistress Ellen Ternan (known as Nelly) and her mother, Frances. They have recently alighted from a train at Shoreham Station as Charles has been overcome by the shakes and has been unable to continue his rail journey.

He never uses his real name in such awkward and complex circumstances. He introduces himself as a Mister Tringham, esquire, accompanied by his god-daughter Nelly and supported by her mother.

"Let me rest awhile in order to dispense of this constant shaking," says Charles as he sits without being asked.

Eliza observing his distress, dispatches Obadiah with all haste to prepare a set of rooms above.

"I cannot have you abroad with such pallor as this gentleman displays. I feel you may all find a benefit in resting a while. You are welcome. You are all most welcome"

Although the day is splendid in heat and the windows thrown open to the skies, when Charles finally sits, he asks the boy to be kind enough to build a fire and take the chill from his ancient bones.

"May I trouble you once more, young…?"

"Obadiah, sir"

"Young Obadiah would you be so kind as to fetch me my overcoat, I believe I have abandoned it below."

As Obadiah retrieves the coat, a manuscript falls from the pocket. It is several unpublished chapters of an excellent story by Mister Charles Dickens called 'Our Mutual Friend'. Obadiah has read the early published chapters but has no recognition of these. He replaces the manuscript in the pocket and returns to the rooms above, knowing that the man can only be one person.

Entering the room, Obadiah notices that the man sits unusually close to the fire.

"Is there something of consequence regarding my appearance?" asks Charles.

"No, sir, it's just that you have the look of a haunted man."

"T'is due to a change in my circumstances, Obadiah, I have just this afternoon escaped from the throats of death. Not far from here was an accident of the most horrific sort, the train in which I travelled left the rails. Pour me a brandy Obadiah. There's a good man."

Obadiah likes being called a man and juggles the word in his head as Charles imbibes the first glass. Empty now, Charles holds the glass out for Obadiah to immediately refill.

In the adjoining room, Nelly is being attended by Eliza and Charlotte. She, too, is explaining their current circumstances as Eliza dresses Nelly's wound to her upper left arm.

"So, you are Mister Tringham's god-daughter?" asks Eliza as a distraction to subdue Nelly's pain.

Nelly sadly replies, "He describes it as such, but it is not the truth."

"I did not mean to breach a threshold with my inquisitiveness."

"You did not Eliza, if anything, you are kindness itself. Mister Tringham is a writer, together with my mother we have spent a French summer in the gentleman's company. He is my companion, not my godfather".

"It is of no consequence to me whatsoever," says an apologetic Eliza, who watches as Charlotte excuse herself from the room.

"May I speak freely?" asks Nelly.

So, Nelly explains that she met Charles when still only eighteen years of age, and he was, even then, an elderly gentleman. She knows that Mister Tringham has a family and that she will be held to account one day, but that day has not yet arrived and whether t'is the pain or the closeness of death she has tasted this day, Ellen Ternan speaks one sentence that will never pass her lips again.

"Our son lies buried in France".

Next door, Obadiah has finished building up the fire to a roar which is almost impotent against the shaking. Obadiah knows this is not the best of times, but he feels compelled to ask:

"I wondered, sir, if it did not burden you too much, that perhaps you could describe the accident?"

"Why should you not be interested? After all, you are a boy."

"I am a man, Mister Tringham". Charles feels terrible, and apologies to Obadiah, then implores him to make himself comfortable.

"I, and my two companions, had boarded the 2.38 tidal-train at Folkestone. All was well abroad, and the world was an excellent container until I felt the carriage shaking, first this way then the other. My little Nell cried out, 'let us all hold hands and die as friends'. A silence followed Obadiah, one that hushed the very birds on the trees. I crawled to the window to observe that our carriage was hanging twenty feet, at least above a ravine held by the slightest of graces. The others had been less fortunate, each having crashed to the river below. I called out to the train guards asking did they recognise me......."

He has said too much.

"You mean did they recognise <u>you,</u> Mister Dickens?"

Charles smiles at the boy. "It is our secret, Mister Dickens."

"Once my two companions were safely at the top of the hill, I returned to the ravine. It would have been less of a chore to have walked into the jaws of hell.

"The valley was awash with the dead and dying. I climbed the side of our train and re-entered our carriage, retrieving my top hat and a brandy flask.

"I filled my hat with water and took it to a young man who lay a short distance from me. What I could see, but he could not, was the fatal damage to his upper head. He asked that I slake his thirst, asked me not to leave him, then closed his eyes for the last time.

"Slightly to the north was a lady of similar age to myself who lay on the ground. I lifted her and sat her against a little pollard tree and wetted her lips with brandy. She smiled at me with one half of her mouth, and I instructed her to wait as I fetched for help. The next time I passed the tree, she had expired. It was then I remembered I had left my manuscript in the pocket of my overcoat, and that was in the carriage we had vacated. I climbed as the carriage threatened to crash along with all the others. Yet, I did not relish rewriting those chapters. I recovered the document, which I am assuming you must have identified."

Charles did not instruct Obadiah on all the facts regarding the three hours he spent tending to the dead and dying. In all, ten people perished, and forty-nine were injured. He could not talk of it to others for fear of the scandal in his choice of companions.

When he asked Obadiah, what would ensure his silence regarding his true identity, Obadiah asked for only one thing, a new story written by the greatest of all writers.

The source of the crash was a deadly simple one: the foreman at the site in Staplehurst had read the wrong timetable. His times were for the following day, the Saturday, when the next train was due shortly after five o'clock but on that day, the 9th of June, Dickens' train was due to pass the bridge at several minutes after three. Thinking that the workmen had two clear hours of maintenance, the foreman instructed the gang to lift the rails.

Shortly after Dickens finished his recounting of the tale, Charles, Frances, and Nelly were on a train to Charing Cross. They were met at the station by Willis, Dickens confidant, who saw the ladies on to their London home at Mornington Crescent.

Charles had intended to return to his family that evening. A family watched over by his sister-in-law Georgina at Gad's Hill in Higham. Still, the shakes overtook him once again, and he spent the night at his London office.

Charles' panic attacks increased over the following years, and once his daughter noted that, he seemed to sink into a trance and relive the day of the crash. His concentration suffered too, and he found it challenging to complete 'Our Mutual Friend'. He brought it to such an abrupt halt that his publisher asked him to think again and extend it. This he did reluctantly, but it was to be the last novel he ever completed.

It was love that kept Charles silent about that day, and it was love that nurtured him in the final years of his life. He died five years to the day of the train crash while writing 'The Mystery of Edwin Drood'.

As for Charles attendance at the crash, there is a postscript by him at the end of 'Our Mutual Friend', and as for the presence of Nelly, there is a letter sent by Dickens to the Station Master at Charing Cross instructing him of Mistress Ternan's lost jewellery at the crash site.

Regarding our Shoreham friends, Eliza's husband Richard came home several months after Dickens' visit, and they settled into running the Crown Public House together; both are buried in Shoreham churchyard.

A few weeks after the crash, a letter was delivered to Obadiah containing a story, true to his word Mister Charles Dickens, the most famous man in all Christendom, had penned a ghost story called 'The Signalman'.

Aunt Charlotte was committed to Bedlam, where she died in 1877. Benedict, the youngest son, took over the running of the Crown and Obadiah, after many years in the Royal Navy, settled in Australia.

And so dear friends, we are almost done with this remembrance, and whether or not you believe my story, I hope it has amused you. I wish each and every one of you a wonderful life.

THE GREAT FILM FIASCO OF SHOREHAM VILLAGE

Now I know you're going to say to me that you've heard this story before – okay, I might have talked about it as having taken place in another village and in another time, but I was only trying to keep the guilty from being named – honest.

It all happened that one summer, the one in 1940 when the world was turned on its head, and the good folks of Kent were waiting on the enemy to turn up at its door.

Let me say from the start that his story isn't to do with the war, well not directly – I will leave those tales to folks who are worthy of telling them – no, this story is to do with Shoreham Village and about certain individuals who were about to try to cheer the village up.

Above the heads of those Shoreham folks that summer, the Battle of Britain was being fought out; friends and neighbours were sent off to war, and so it fell to one Ichabod Swithin to shoulder the burden of keeping the morale high within the parish.

Ichabod had tossed and turned several nights trying to think of some darned good idea that would be worthy of Shoreham and its inhabitants. He had once been a pianist and tune-smith for some of the well-known stage stars in the early 1900s and thought that perhaps a revival might be on the cards. However, when Ichabod went looking for his old chums, he found that they were either dead or too old to tread the boards.

Ichabod almost gave up in his quest to lift the spirits of his Shoreham family – when one warm Saturday, his grandson, Samuel, came calling. The two of them were best of pals and enjoyed a pint of ale in the Crown, followed by a walk along the river – and it was here that Samuel let it be known to his grandfather that what he was doing was all 'hush-hush' and that he was enjoying it immensely.

Samuel asked his granddad why the old rascal was looking so glum, and Ichabod told him all about the problem he had with trying to cheer the village up.

"What if I could get you a film to show," said Samuel.

"Like what?" Asked his grandfather.

Ichabod thought that perhaps they could show a few Charlie Chaplin reels and a cup of tea to follow. Surely that would do the trick. But Samuel had grander ideas.

"It would mean us getting our hands on a large projector, and perhaps you could hang a large sheet from the stage," said his grandson.

And that, dear folks, is how it happened. The following Friday evening was the allocated date, and the film was to be shown to the good folks of Shoreham for a penny each.

Like all things in life, the best-laid plans (and all that) went slightly off course.

Samuel had done Ichabod proud and had got his hands on a very famous film to show (it helped that Samuel worked in the propaganda department of the war effort – where they made movies to bolster the good people of Britain). The film was Gone with The Wind, and it had only been released in Britain several weeks earlier.

The problem – and it was a problem – was that the film was four hours long, and no one had that amount of time to spend – not with farming, feeding families and a war going on above their heads.

So, it was decided by the council that they would show it in two parts: two hours on the Friday and two hours on the Saturday. That seemed like a practical solution, and so everyone was happy.

That is, until the word got out, up and down the valley, that a great film like Gone with The Wind was showing for a penny in Shoreham.

The queue reached from the village hall to the railway station (which, to those who don't know, the place is about half a mile). There were many disgruntled people that night – and what hurt Ichabod was that many who had gained entry to the film-showing weren't from Shoreham.

Samuel came up with a plan to show the film in two parts the following Friday and Saturday. Ichabod was happy with that wonderful suggestion, as were the rest of the council.

Here is where it gets tricky – there was a big queue, if not a bigger one, on the Saturday night, and some who got in hadn't seen the first part – and some had seen both parts. You'd think that would keep some of the people happy – you'd think – but no, folks started using the fact that they'd seen the Saturday night half to their advantage.

The first incident was when Old George Smith (who had been to the film on Friday) punched his best pal (who had been to the Friday and Saturday showing) in the face when he threatened to tell him the ending of the film.

The next big upset was when Egbert Cuthbert stood up in church the following day and told the congregation that if they didn't give him the contents of the collection plates, he'd tell them all how the film finished. Big Sam, the farmer, managed to grab Egbert and throw him out the building before he got around to telling the good people anything important.

One masked man (everyone guessed it was Egbert again) was found to stand in the High Street and ask for money, or else he'd tell them the whole of the story. Mrs Lupin battered the robber over the head with the Margaret Mitchell novel and said she'd already read Gone with The Wind, thank you very much, and she hurriedly moved on.

Some of the Friday/Saturday night people were seen to huddle in little groups in the village shops and butchers – and they would look over at those who hadn't seen the whole film with a look of pity.

If ever there was a way to divide a village, this was it, and it wasn't what Ichabod had wanted.

Things only got worse the following weekend when they showed part one again – but there was an air raid on the Saturday, and the whole thing was cancelled.

And that is why some folks are still not talking to each other in Shoreham – and why Ichabod ended up with a ninety-five-year-old tap dancer and Ichabod on the piano in the village hall.

It might not be Hollywood but frankly, who's giving a damn.

UNCLE BERTIE

"Bertie is, as Bertie does", was what my Auntie Clara used to say just before she would laugh so hard that a bubble would form at the bottom of her nose. Then she would hold her sides and say, "one more laugh, and I might just wet my knickers".

Uncle Bertie had always been the crazy one of the family, or as my mother - his sister - would say, "one day they will lock him up, I swear to God, and throw away the key".

His first foray into attempting to get to the Tower of London was the day of Queen Victoria's funeral. The village of Shoreham was understandably sad, and Uncle Bertie decided to dress up as a young Victoria and parade up and down Church Street.

One spinster called Victoria was so shocked by what she saw through the window that she took the vapours and lay in a darkened room for several days. It didn't seem to worry the family just how well Uncle Bertie portrayed a woman and a royal one at that.

It was in 1906 that Uncle Bertie and Aunt Clara became custodians of the Kings Arms local hostelry. Aunt Clara's father had made money in some South African mines and had left his wealth to her (he thought Uncle Bertie 'a buffoon' and made sure all the money was in his daughter's name).

Although there was much competition in the village with the public houses, namely The George, The Rising Sun, The Royal Oak, The Two Brewers, and The Crown, they still managed to make a living.

People came in from Swanley and Bromley to see Uncle Bertie and Aunt Clara behind the bar. Sometimes Uncle Bertie would get so drunk that he'd get Aunt Clara to play her fiddle while he danced naked on the table.

Uncle Bertie was forever getting into trouble.

When Christopher Landtrap came to stay in the village, he chose the Kings Arms as his drinking den. He brought down many 'artistic' London types who would quaff ale and sing songs down by the river. Christopher claimed to be a grandson of Samuel Palmer, the Shoreham artist, it was neither proved nor disproved, but Shoreham being Shoreham, no one disputed the fact.

Early in 1910, Christopher got caught up in the photography bug which had spread amongst the bright young things.

Christopher decided to make a record of all the

public houses in Shoreham and that he would start with the Kings Arms. Uncle Bertie asked

Christopher how long it took to take a photograph, and he told him that it would take sixty seconds. So when Christopher asked everyone to stay indoors while he took a photograph – everyone did - except Uncle Bertie, who ran into the street just as the photo was being taken.
This photo stands today.

Uncle Bertie died in London when a Zeppelin dropped a bomb in the street where he was walking, and Auntie Clara died as she listened to Elvis Presley on the radio.

GLENN MILLER AND SHOREHAM

My grandmother used to say that the village, meaning Shoreham, would find you, take you in, scrub you up and only let you go when you were a happier, smiling person.

I mention this because it may have some bearing on the story I am about to tell you. As usual, please don't blame me. I am only repeating what my grandmother told my grandfather – just before he said, 'stop talking stupid, Annie' and went to the Rising Sun for an ale.

For the sake of the story, I have to take you back to the winter of 1944, when things were a lot different from what they are today.

The war had been raging for several years, and most people had just got on with things. My grandmother, as well as bringing up her family, was a cleaner in and around Shoreham. On a Tuesday, she would help out at the Old George at the top of Church Street. It was here that she met a young French girl, Eloise, who had probably been on this Earth twenty summers at the time. The two women hit it off immediately and became best pals.

One cold, snowy December morning, a ray of sunshine walked into my grandmother's life. The Hollywood actor, David Niven, returned home for the war and took part in the Allied invasion of Normandy earlier that year. He would sometimes drop into the George on the way to, or from, London. He told my grandmother once that he was based in Chilham, and that was as much as he could tell her. It wasn't until years later that she found out he had been in some Signal's Unit or another when she read one of his autobiographies.

The rascal smote both my grandmother and Eloise and had things been different, Niven might have been my grandfather. One morning on his way back to his Kent village, David Niven stopped by the George for a chat. David asked my grandmother if Eloise was about – but apparently, she was at the Co-operative shop on the High Street – so they made a date for that evening for all three of them, and a pal of David's, to meet in a tea-room at the other end of the village.

My grandmother had a million-and-one errands to run before their tea-time meeting. On the other hand, Eloise spent the rest of the day borrowing what little make-up there was, painting stockings on her legs and generally looking like a beautiful young French girl.

In the end, my grandmother never got to that tea-time meeting, for she was too busy mending and re-mending clothes that belonged to my mother and her brother. Like most women and men during the war years, my grandmother never stopped working to repair and make-do.

The next time Eloise ran into my grandmother, the French girl had a bounce in her step and a smile that almost cut her face in two. Apparently, the American gentleman whom David had introduced to Eloise had been the most excellent companion.

"So funny, Annie, and so clever. He is a musician," Eloise told my grandmother. Even after all these years, my grandmother couldn't understand why it hadn't twigged at the time who the man was.

Eloise, David, and the man all went out for drinks in the city, and over the following weeks, my grandmother saw less and less of Eloise. That was until that chilly afternoon in November when my mother had taken a few minutes from her day to walk up by the Cross. It gave her a sense of perspective walking up there:

"It would keep me going for the rest of the day," she would say, and it was up there that she first met the American gentleman. My grandmother said he was a lot older than Eloise, but that wasn't unusual in those days of the war. Younger men were thin on the ground back then.

"He kept humming little tunes, and then he'd giggle in that American way before kissing the French girl. I think he was married. He never really talked about his family," said my grandmother.

It was a day in early December when my grandmother entered the George public house to find Eloise crying in the corner of one of the bars.

Eloise told my grandmother that the American gentleman had fallen madly, totally, head-over-heels in love with her and that she felt the same.

"He wants us to go away, except...he is in the army, and he must do what he is told," Eloise said. "He will either be killed, or he must go back to America, to his...family."

My grandmother said that Eloise was heartbroken.

December the 13th was the last time my grandmother saw Eloise or her American friend. My grandmother received a postcard at Christmas that year from Scarborough in Yorkshire – the card just said 'Merci. Eloise'.

It was probably around the same time that my grandmother heard about a famous musician who had disappeared over the English Channel on his way to France. The photo in the newspaper was the same man she had met with Eloise up by the Cross that day.

Or at least it looked like him. My grandmother was convinced it was Glenn Miller that she had met that day.

The weird thing was David Niven was Miller's best buddy in England and apparently had drinks with him the night before he disappeared – but he never mentioned any of it in his autobiography. My grandmother had bought a copy to see if she, or Eloise, or Shoreham were ever mentioned – but they hadn't.

Like everyone else, my grandmother just got on with her life. Sometimes, when she had a ginger wine or two, she'd tell folks of her meeting in Shoreham with David Niven. Once or twice, she thought about telling the story of Glenn Miller – but she would always change her mind.

She'd just raise a glass to the French girl and smile.

THE YEAR OF SMILING AGAIN

The year after the war was one of the strangest in Alfred's life. Even now, looking back through the years, he still got shivers running down his back when he thought of those days.

That was when summers stretched from one end of the year to the next, when holidays lasted a lifetime when perfection was always in front of you, and it was never questioned.

Ever since his father, Andrew, had gone off to war, Alfred would sit up at the Cross-on-the-Hill watching as far as the railway station, knowing that one day his dad would come home to the family. Yet the war had been over for a long time, and the only thing he understood was from the screwed-up telegram that he had found in a corner: 'missing in action', it said. Only three little words, but they had the power to change lives.

Alfred's mother had been working for some time at the Rising Sun. It was one of the more popular public houses in the village, and it had proved popular with the soldiers billeted in Shoreham during the war. She was happy in that place, and she worked hard, scrubbing, cleaning, and keeping her thoughts under control. There was the odd tear in the cellar when no one was looking but compared with some of the other families in the village, hers was a lighter burden. She had her boy, Alfred, who had been a Godsend. He was just like his father, strong and sensible. He had taken on the mantle of man-of-the-house, and it fitted him well. Yet she knew Alfred had his sad times too, and she would often see him sitting up at the Cross just as the sun was going down.

Some days, he waited at the railway station watching everyone and anyone who got off the trains, and on those days when he returned home, he would say nothing, go to his room and then she could hear him sobbing. It broke her heart every time.

On the odd occasion, Greta, Alfred's mother, would be asked to help out at the Rising Sun in the evenings, perhaps for a celebration of a new life or for a remembrance of a life well-lived.

On those nights, she would take Alfred with her, and he would settle in the back room with a good book and a nice cool lemonade. Alfred was a curious boy and would peek through the keyhole at the Rising Sun's customers. He would watch some of them change from sad to happy, and others would go in the opposite direction, he wasn't sure what part beer had to play in all of this, but he found it all exciting. His father liked to drink beer, and he wondered if it made him happy or sad.

There was one particular customer – Jazz, as everyone called him, but Alfred doubted if that was his real name. He was a large Canadian who had come for the War and had stayed. He rented the large cottage on Church Street, and he planned to marry Agnes, a young English girl who worked in a shop in London and who had stolen Jazz' heart.

Opposite the Rising Sun was the clearest of little rivers, and across it was a bridge where Alfred liked to sit and watch the fish while waiting on his mother finishing her shift at the pub. On their way home, Alfred would run into the Kings Arms and collect a pie or some cheese from Rita, Greta's pal. Rita had lost her husband in France.

And in their stories lies the truth of villages. For much of the time – in peacetime, that is – villages can be claustrophobic and full of busybodies who should mind their own business, thank you very much. But in the dark days when a helping hand or a kind work is very much-needed, it is in those days that the strength and purpose of a little village can be found. Inseparable since their days at Shoreham Primary School, Rita and Greta helped and gave each other strength (and pie when it was called for).

One afternoon, instead of sitting on the bridge and because of the increasing heat of the day, Alfred sat down by the river and cooled himself on the breeze that was blowing between the bridge arches.

"You Alfie?" Came this booming voice.

To Alfred's ear, which was now tuned to accents after the number of soldiers who had passed through Shoreham, he knew it was Canadian rather than American. Standing all 6 feet 4 inches above him was Jazz and Agnes, his English sweetheart.

"You're Greta's kid, ain't cha?"

Alfred was taken back at first since no one had called him kid before, and it felt good. People only talked like this in films.

"Alfred," said the boy who stood to shake hands with Jazz.

"Well, would cha look at that. You have manners, boy." And with that handshake, Jazz and Alfred (or Alfie as he was known after that) became the firmest of friends.

It warmed Greta's heart when she looked out of the Rising Sun window to see her son sitting on the bridge and fishing with his Canadian pal. Something good was happening to him. He had stopped visiting the railway station so often, and on some beautiful sun-filled mornings, she found her son smiling. It had been so long, too long since he'd done so.

Even Rita had found a skip in her step. She was walking out with a teacher from Bromley. She felt guilty at times, considering she was a war widow, but as Greta had told her, it had been six years since James had died, and she needed to smile again, too.

One autumn afternoon, when Jazz and Alfie were looking for rabbits up in the woods above the village, Jazz said he needed to have a seat as he wasn't young anymore. He seemed old to Alfie in those days, but he was probably only in his early thirties.

"You, Alfie are the luckiest kid alive," said the big booming Canadian voice. "You have the sweetest mama; you live in the prettiest village I have ever seen, and there is everything a kid could want here to grow up happy. I know you ain't seen your Pa for the longest of times, but you keep the faith, and the world will turn from good to perfect."

Then Jazz reached into his pocket and pulled out a Canadian coin. He flipped it in the air and caught it on the back of his hand.

"Now I ain't sure if it is 'heads' or 'tails', but I want you to call it, and if the universe wants you to have the coin, you'll call it right."

"Heads," said Alfie and 'heads' it was which meant that Jazz handed over the coin to his friend.

"It'll give you one wish," said Jazz with a huge grin on his face. "At least, it worked for me," then he winked at Alfie.

"See Alfie, my Grandmother back in Canada gave me that coin, and she told me the same story. I didn't believe her at first, but she swore to me it was true. She said it would keep me safe in the War, and it did funnily enough because I found a way to get two wishes out of it. I squeezed the coin in my palm, and I said that I wanted to find the love of my life after the fighting was over. That meant I had to stay safe and get to meet the sweetest girl in the whole world."

Then Jazz let rip with the biggest and happiest of laughs as the two of them made their way off the hills with rabbits slung over their shoulders.

Alfie thought long and hard about his wish. The basic one was easy; he wanted his Dad home and back with the family, but what if he wanted to try for two wishes, just like Jazz. What if he wished that they all went on holiday together as a family, then he'd get everyone back and get a holiday.

So early one morning, he went up onto the hill next to the Cross and squeezed the coin in the palm of his hand and wished that he and his family would go on holiday.

Then Alfie waited and waited a little more.

It was the Spring of 1947, and nothing had been heard of his Alfie's father, and they were no nearer to going on holiday. So, one day in passing over the bridge going to meet his mother, he threw the coin into the river and with it his childhood.

By 1948, Greta had started to talk to a racing driver from Brands Hatch, who used to stop by at the Rising Sun. She helped serve, from time to time, when it started to get busy. His name was Jack, and he drove for a team. Within six months Greta and Jack were married, and although Alfie was pleased for his mother, he never gave up on seeing his father again. Jazz moved back to Canada with his new wife, and his parting shot was asking Alfie if he still had the coin. Alfie nodded but felt guilty at lying.

"And when you have kids, Alfie, you can pass the coin on to them."

Alfie's life became more exciting, and Jack would take the boy to Brands Hatch to sit in the racing cars. He decided that racing was probably the life for him too.

One day when he was sitting on the bridge waiting for his mother, he noticed a glint of sun reflecting off the bottom of the nearly dry river. When he investigated further, he found it was the coin he'd thrown away. He stuck it in his sock and promised himself he would never throw it away again.

A couple of weeks later, Jack, Greta and Alfie went on holiday to Jersey in the Channel Islands. It was the best holiday that Alfie could remember, and he also remembered it for one other reason, it was on the second Saturday that he heard his mother laughing out loud, not just chuckling but laughing from the bottom of her heart.

Life didn't always work out the way you wished, but sometimes it worked out the way you needed.

As old Alf sits in the back garden thinking back over the years when he was a boy in Shoreham, he smiles.

They are all gone now, but he did get to see his father's grave, which was located in late 1965.

Sometimes when you are in the middle of things, they don't make sense until much later. Alf looks over at his grandchildren playing in the garden.

"Robbie," as Alfie calls the eldest over.

"Have you still got that coin your daddy gave you, the one I gave him?"

"I do, Grandad."

"Have you made your wish yet?"

"Not yet, Grandad."

"Did I ever tell you about a man called Jazz who said you could get two wishes from it...."

SHOREHAM AND THE GEESE

Most of her 94 years had been spent in this beautiful little corner of the world. The rear of her property looked up to the Cross on the hill above, and now that most of her days were spent resting in bed – she found this a favourable view. In the Spring and the Summer months, she watched the little birds and then the wild geese as they came to visit in her back yard and the fields beyond.

It hadn't always been this way. In her younger, vibrant days, she worked on the farm and later in the Cooperative shop on the village High Street.

She had been born into a place that had meant the most happiness and, therefore, had never wanted to leave. She had been married for a short time, there had been no children, but she had accepted that fact and moved on with her life. Her husband had always wanted sons and daughters and had eventually found a family with his second wife in Hastings.

In all her 94 years, much of it had been spent looking from her window on to the passers-by and their changing tastes and fashions – and as the older residents had aged and passed on, so the village constantly invigorated itself with newer, younger dynamic families. Most of these folks now worked in the city and spent much of their time commuting. She had been lucky. She had found everything she needed within reach. Not many had had that chance.

But the main thing that preoccupied her thoughts was the magic in this little haven. Her great grandmother, a woman who had been there at the opening of the Co-op shop – in the same year that Queen Victoria had died – had always told her the same sentence over and over again, 'Shoreham finds you, you don't find Shoreham'.

She had always wondered what that had meant – but it wasn't about the likes of herself or her family. It was about the souls who thought they had discovered this hamlet by accident – a lucky accident – but an accident all the same.

Yet she knew the truth. They came here incomplete, or sad, or single, or unhappily married, or sick, or healthy, or hopeful, or lost – and they stayed long enough to put things right in their lives. To find that special person, or to lose the wrong one. To beat the depression or some disease or another.

To raise a family or find a new one. To see the end of loneliness in the company of new friends or to find confidence when it was lacking.

Whatever their needs, Shoreham grabbed them as

they passed by, then dusted them down and didn't let go until the time was right for them to move on.

She had seen it time and time again – enough to know that it wasn't a fluke but a certainty – a miracle.

It was a truth that not everyone came to the village searching for something, but most did. They just didn't know it. And from her little window on the High Street, she had watched them find it and had taken comfort in their happiness and their newfound lives.

Now from her bedroom window, she watched as the geese came to the field beyond the trees.

Those beautiful birds waited on her to close her eyes for the very last time, and then they carried her soul to that far country where she could rest.

SHOREHAM ROSE

Perhaps I should start way back at the beginning.

The first time I laid eyes on Sally – Ludlow as she was called then – she had a permanent band-aid on a pair of National Health spectacles. She was nothing special, at least not to me. She was just one of those children who run through the streets of Shoreham on any given sunny evening. Kent, back then, was a different place than it is today.

It was a gentler, kinder time and in the years after the war, there was still rationing, but with that came a feeling that we had to look after one another.

Sally and her family lived on the High Street, and we lived on a small farm on the back road. On those summer evenings, the kids used to meet up by the Cross on the hill. The Cross had been cut out of the chalk hills in the years after the Great War to remember those who had given their lives, and by a strange irony, it had to be covered up during World War 2 as the enemy bombers used it as a landmark.

That night, the night it happened – we both must have been about fifteen back then – I was sitting on the hill overlooking the village, and I knew that when the lantern came on outside the Rising Sun pub, it was time for me to head over the hill and back to the farm.

I loved this view, and even on a warm evening, there would still be smoke rising from the chimneys and leaving a ghostly drift across the valley. The smell of the grass and the fields and the fires were like nowhere else on earth.
"Is it okay if I sit?"

And there she was, Sally, standing over me as she pushed those spectacles back up her nose. They always seemed to be trying to escape her face.
"Well?"
"Sure", I said to the funny little girl wearing the funny little glasses.
"I always see you sitting up here from my bedroom window."
"It's the best place in the world to sit", I said.
"My father doesn't like me watching you."
"Why?" I knew I was going to regret asking this.
"He says you're a weird one, always on your own."
"And you, what do you think?" I asked.
"Oh, I don't think you're weird. I love you."

And that was that. That was the night, the first time, a person other than my grandmother, told me that they loved me.

The rest of the summer, we were inseparable, and even her father got to like me. When I wasn't working on our farm, I was over at Sally's, and some days she would come and help at our place. The night before we were due to go back to school, she made a small ring from the grass on the hill and asked me to propose to her.

"Sally Ludlow, will you marry me?"

She said 'yes'.

"And you can't ever get out of it, James. Till death, us do part."

At fifteen years of age, Sally and I were engaged to be married. Sally said we should start saving right away to have a big wedding and invite all the family. She reckoned we'd be very old by the time we could afford it.

"Maybe nineteen or twenty." That seemed such a long way away.

Every penny I earned went into our secret wedding box, and it lay side by side with Sally's contributions. Of course, we were going to get married in St. Peter and St. Paul's, the local church.

Then Sally moved to High Wycombe. It seemed her grandmother was poorly, and her family wanted to live with her.

"It'll only be a few weeks", she said.

But it wasn't. It was almost a year. I met Sally in London on two occasions, but we decided to write to each other instead as we were saving our money.

To start with, we wrote every day, but eventually, it was one small note, once a week. I almost gave up and thought she was never coming back.

Then I got called up for National Service, and I was shipped out to Aden. Before I left, I heard that Sally's father was coming back to Shoreham to work in the butcher shop at the corner of Crown Road and that Sally and her mother would follow on.

Her father rented a room above the butcher's while he waited on his family, but since his mother-in-law was in a state of decline, his wife and daughter stayed on in High Wycombe.

I came back home twice, but there wasn't any time to travel to see Sally as I was needed on the farm.

By the time Sally and I were in Shoreham, she was accompanied by her boyfriend, Andrew. He was studying to be a doctor, and his family were something in High Wycombe, leastways that's what her mother told me. I don't think she meant anything by it.

Sally and her parents moved temporarily into the Station Master's house at Shoreham as the wife of the house and Sally's mother were the best of friends. Every time I called at the station, I was told that Sally was out, but I'm sure I saw the curtains twitch in a room upstairs. I wrote to her a couple of times but never got any reply.

That year my family decided to send me off to Agricultural college in deepest Sussex, and this allowed me to return from time to time to work on the farm. I had a few girlfriends while I was studying, but none of them was ever Sally. She was always in my thoughts one way or another. Then one day, I ran into Sally's mother, who told me that her daughter had married and moved to High Wycombe.

That's one of those moments in your life when you feel as if everything inside you has been ripped out, and yet you still manage to function – I continued to speak to her mother without missing a beat.

I threw myself into working on the farm, and from time to time, I got involved in the Village Players: a drama group that helped me take my mind off of Sally.

Once a week, I would meet up with pals in The Royal Oak, the best of all pubs in Shoreham, and that was my life for the next ten years.

It was at a wedding in the new golf club that our paths crossed again. Sally hadn't aged in all those years; she was still as beautiful as ever, but there was a sadness on her face.

"Hi" was all she said, and how long had I waited on that?
She had nursed her husband for the last three years, and he'd died just before Christmas. This was a grown-up Sally I was talking to. She was only back for a weekend to remind herself how beautiful Shoreham was as a village. She had begun to think she'd dreamt the place up.

I told her that she could stay on our farm the next time she was in the village. She said thanks and told me she'd think about it, but she had to get back to her family. She had an eight-year-old daughter and a five-year-old son, and she had to work out what her future was going to hold.

Then the following summer, she came for a weekend with the kids to stay on the farm, and that was the happiest I had been in years. She, too, looked less sad.

What can I tell you?

We married the following year, and we set up house in one of the farm cottages.
We had one further child between us, Simon and

the five of us had the best of times. Sure, we struggled, but I was with Sally and my family, and anything was possible.

The older boy, James and the girl, Sue, moved into London, and both had families of their own. Simon settled down and took over the farm, letting me and Sally travel for the first time. We even drove across the States.
Sally left me in her 65th year – she had been ill for several months, and her leaving took my heart. Sure, the kids and the grandchildren visited the farm, but once again, I spent my days missing Sally.

When I felt strong enough to clear out her clothes, I found a small box in the back of the wardrobe and in it was the small ring made from grass. She'd kept it all those years.

When the time comes, I'm going to be buried in the church next to Sally.

It'll just be me and her again.

Shoreham Rose – the song on YouTube:

https://www.youtube.com/watch?v=0QnHQsV9-IU&t=9s

THE SHOREHAM VILLAGE HALL HOOTENANNY

As she was putting up the posters on the village shop wall, she realised that she wasn't too sure what a 'Hootenanny' was. Like everything else in life these days, she had to ask her grandchildren. The two kids looked at each other the way they did when she said she'd like to learn to use a 'Lex Box'.

They had both tutted and corrected her that it was an 'X Box'.

"So, what is a Hootenanny, then?" She asked them. "And could you hand me that drawing pin? Thank you."

Emily, the eldest of the two, informed their Grandmother that it was a music get-together.

"A mash-up, Gran." Said James.

She smiled but was none the wiser.

What it was, was a party at the end of it all. She knew that much. What we had all come through over the past months deserved a party.

Life was life, she supposed, but in a village, it was strange and extraordinary at the same time, like living in a big city but with all the oxygen taken out. People were closer in all sorts of senses in a village.

They bumped off each other. They all had to share the same limited oxygen.

The weirdest thing about all those Lockdowns – and it was comforting to talk about them in the past – had been the way you had to face up to things. We had all been so busy living that most of us hadn't noticed how little we had taken care of ourselves. Or how empty our lives could be when we were not running around. For some, it spurred them on to learn, or paint, or sing, or dance, or run naked around their back garden. For others, it was looking into an unkind mirror every day. Some souls crumbled – perhaps we all did.

So that was why the village was having this party. To celebrate the fact that most of us had made it through and to remember those hearts who hadn't. Many souls were still suffering the long-term effects of it all. They needed the party more than most.

She finally got the last of the posters up and stood back and looked at her handy-work. They had been produced by several of the folks in the village. That's what this life was – sharing and helping each other.

It was also what the village hall was all about. She had appeared in plays, in pantos, in cabarets and hadn't been very good in any of them – but then who cared? You came to the village hall and left your troubles – and her case, her talent at the door.

That night, the night of the Hootenanny, was like no other she had experienced in the village in all the years she had lived there. It was all free, of course, and everyone brought something.

One of the men brought his orchestra, his brother and friends decorated the hall. Some brought things they had made, or knitted, or painted. They were proudly splashed around the walls. One retired plumber brought his homemade hooch and regretted it.

The ones who wanted to sing got up and did so. Others just danced in the corners. And for the first time in a very long time, people hugged. People kissed each other – some more than was necessary – but hey, it was a party.

And as she looked around the hall, she noticed what it was that made living in a village special. Everyone brought something of themselves to the party.

Folks simply ignored the time and danced through the night. It was as the summer sun was rising that the last of them left the village hall. They would all come back later and clean up. It could wait.

She stood watching the stragglers all heading home, still laughing and joking and hugging and kissing.

She smiled contentedly to herself. She realised that life had become wonderful again.

COMING HOME

When he stepped from the train, there was still heat in the air. He could smell the fields and the soil, and as he looked across the platform, he was sure he could see his father walking up to the station to meet him. But like everything else in his life, they were all gone a long time ago.

He'd been back for his father's death, of course, and he had thought about all the things they would say to each other in the final hours – but his father had slipped away with only a smile and soft squeeze of his son's hand.

He lifted his rucksack over his shoulder and headed down the stairs to Station Road. Things were still very much the same. The road was a little newer, and the hedges looked a little different from what he remembered, but it was still home. In the field, he could imagine his mother waving back from all those years ago. Smiling and alive, not touched by the bad ending.

He could see the light in the window of the Rectory. There would be a new vicar living there now – one he didn't know. He had lived through three vicars, and all of them had helped him at difficult times in his life. Whatever was said, the village needed a church and a vicar. It was somewhere to be thought of as unique.

As he turned the corner, he held his breath. There was the Old George – with maybe a little more painted makeup, a little more front but still the same old place. He and his pals had drunk there, perhaps a little earlier than the law would have allowed, but that was living in a small village. There had been a family who had owned it for as long as he could remember. It was easy to forget, as a child running in and out of the place, that it was someone's home as well as a bar.

A couple of walkers were sitting enjoying an ale as he passed by, so he stopped and watched. The Old George had been inviting folks to sit and rest for a long, long time now; the farmers, the bikers, the musicians, the Morris dancers, all had sat and supped; all had talked about their lives and loves, all had discussed their troubles – all were gone now.

The church gate was still as he had remembered that day when it had been decked with flowers for his sister's wedding. Her body lay in the churchyard now – it had done for some seventeen years.

He turned past Church Cottages and into Church Street – he was sure he remembered a shop in that street, but his memory came and went these days. It was hard to be sure of what had been and what was the tainted memories of an old man.

As he walked down the street, he could see the dying Sun reflecting on the river, and it made him feel the way it always had. It made him feel warm inside, just like a good whisky. He had sat by the river, man and boy, and it had been the one constant in his life.

Two children were trying to catch fish from the bridge, just like he had done back then, and like him, the kids were pulling up empty hooks. But it was the comradeship, the feeling of safety, the feeling of a village watching over you while you fished that had kept him happy as a child. Nowhere else in the world had he ever felt as safe and happy as he had on those days as a boy sitting on the bridge – fishing.

The Sun had seemed warmer and brighter back then. Probably another trick of his old mind. He turned to look back at where the Rising Sun pub had been. Some nights he would sit by the river waiting on his father to come out of the 'Sun and bring him a lemonade.

"Cheers, dad," he'd say, and his Dad would ruffle his hair. Just to do that once again, he thought – just once.

Folks were eating outside the King's Arms – a new generation of people from London and all the areas in between, having a day in the country. That was the village's lifeblood – visitors, it kept the pubs and the world turning.

The school – ah, the school. That was where he was happy. Happy childhood had been formed – where his friendships had been forged. It had been the best of days, and nothing in his later life was ever as brilliant.

He turned the corner into the High Street – the Royal Oak pub, where his grandparents had met their friends on a Friday night, was a beautiful private house now. He supposed that people didn't meet in pubs anymore, the way they once did, there were other ways to socialise now. The Oak had been the first pub he had been taken to, and it had been by his Granddad who had bought him his first beer. Boy, it had tasted good, and he licked his lips as he had done all those years ago.

Up ahead, he could see the Two Brewers. It had changed. It was a sophisticated bar/restaurant now; back then, it was where all the bad boys and girls had hung out. They weren't awful, just young people trying to get a handle on life and enjoying themselves in the process.

He noticed some new houses and some revived old ones nudging the High Street as he continued along. The Cooperative shop had gone – that was where his mother had worked and his

Grandmother. It had been an exciting place to hang about, especially at Christmas. He could still remember the smells of that place. The wonderful, beautiful smells.

The allotments were still on the right, still bursting with colours, and plants and love. As he got to the top of Crown Road, it all came rushing back; his pals, the games, the running up and down the road – they were the best, the very best, of times.

The Crown pub hadn't changed, either. This was where he had met the girls and his buddies in his older days. It was a beautiful pub inside and out, and as he thought back, and although his face was sporting a smile, there was still a warm tear on his cheek.

Perhaps the saddest thing is going back, going home, and finding that it has changed all too much – but not this place. Coming home to this place was a pleasure. It was a village that had changed little, sure the people were different, and some of the buildings were painted brighter or had been pulled down – but the village was still the village.

He thought he might head over to the school field and look at the place where he had scored that goal – the one which folks had talked about for months. He remembered how everyone in the Royal Oak had bought him a beer because of it. He had played for the village football team but had dreamed of playing, one day, for a big London club. It wasn't to be.

There is a saying that if you want to give God a laugh, tell him what your plans are. Nothing had worked out the way he'd hoped, but he had been luckier than most folks – he had known a place of love, life, and safety. He had the happiest days of his existence in this village and perhaps the saddest days too – but folks had rallied around – everyone had helped, and in the end, he had moved on and moved away.

As he walked towards the school field, he stopped and sat a while outside the village hall. There were worse places to have lived, he thought. He looked over at the little village he had called home, and then he wept. Wept buckets.

For everything and everyone.

Little Shoreham Stories

Printed in Great Britain
by Amazon